DANNY ORLIS
AND A
TEENAGE MARRIAGE

DANNY ORLIS

AND A

TEENAGE MARRIAGE

BERNARD PALMER

Danny Orlis and a Teenage Marriage
© 2024 by Bernard Palmer
All rights reserved. First edition 1967.
Second edition 2024.

Cover image: Adobe Firefly

Character illustrations: John Ball

Editor: Jon D. Fogdall

Aneko Press *Youth*

www.anekopress.com

Aneko Press, Life Sentence Publishing, and our logos are trademarks of Life Sentence Publishing, Inc.
203 E. Birch Street
P.O. Box 652
Abbotsford, WI 54405

JUVENILE FICTION / Religious / Christian / Action & Adventure

Paperback ISBN: 979-8-88936-038-4

eBook ISBN: 979-8-88936-039-1

10 9 8 7 6 5 4 3 2 1

Available where books are sold

CONTENTS

ALEX SEEKS A JOB

It was a warm spring afternoon in Fairview, Minnesota. The last of the snow had melted and the roads were dry and firm once more. Grass was greening and new leaves were clothing the birch and poplar in the forest. Kids were beginning to play baseball on the vacant lots around town and fishermen were finding excuses to leave work early.

Robin Smith hummed a happy little tune as she set the supper table.

"You sure sound happy tonight," Alex said.

She smiled up at him.

"And why shouldn't I?"

He came up behind her and encircled her waist with his arm.

"I didn't know my getting a job would make such a difference to you," he said.

She pivoted to face him. "I am happy you've got a chance of getting a job, Alex. I can't deny that."

"You and me both." His grin widened. "I've about had it up to here living in this crummy joint. When I get to work, one of the first things I'm going to do is see that we get a better apartment."

"Oh, Alex."

"Yeh. I've been thinking about one of those new apartments – you know the ones the girls all talk about."

"Park Lane?"

"That's the place. We'll get an apartment there." Her face grew serious.

"We'd never be able to afford an apartment there, Alex," she told him.

"Who says we won't?"

"But they're so expensive."

"So what? We'll have some money coming in."

Slowly she pulled away from him and went back to setting the table.

They had been happy in their little apartment, but it would be nice to have a better place. One where the wallpaper was new and the front door didn't stick.

"I don't figure on pumping gas all my life," Alex told her. "I was thinking about it a little while ago. I can learn how to operate a gas station if I get this job. Then we can get a little money together and I can have a station of my own." He wrote down some figures on the back of an envelope. "By the time we're 30 years old I can have a string of service stations, and maybe a good motel."

"That would be wonderful."

"You know, I might just stay in the service station business, if I like it."

"Do you think you'll get the job?"

"I don't know, but I've got a good chance of getting it. Dad stopped at the Highway Service Station this afternoon to get his car greased. Mr. Pearson told him one of his men quit today and he's shorthanded. So, I called him on the phone and he said for me to come in and see him tomorrow morning."

She stared at him as though it could not quite be true.

"Did he talk–." She stopped and began again. "Did he sound encouraging?"

"Just about as encouraging as a guy could sound over the telephone. He said I was the first application he'd had and he wants to see me. You couldn't ask for anything more than that."

She finished taking up their evening meal and they sat down across from each other.

"It would be so wonderful not to have to depend on our parents for everything."

"You can say that again." He picked up his fork and toyed with it thoughtfully. "When I start thinking about all we've cost them in the last few months it makes me want to hurry and get a good job so we can start doing things for them."

Robin bowed her head to ask the blessing. Before she could speak Alex stopped her.

"I haven't done too much praying in my life," he broke in, the tone in his voice changing suddenly. "But if there's anything to it, you'd better pray now." His handsome young face became even more serious. "I've just got to get this job, Robin. I don't think I've ever wanted anything half so bad."

Her heart sang.

It had happened. It had actually happened.

Alex asked her to pray about something. That showed he wasn't as hard and indifferent to the gospel as he tried to pretend he was. It wouldn't be long until he would be going to church and Sunday school regularly with her. Then he would get saved. And that would mean more to her than the job, a Park Lane apartment, or anything else in all the world.

That night they lay awake for a long while talking about the service station job he was going to see about.

The following morning Alex was up an hour earlier than usual. He took a shower and put on his suit, white shirt, and tie.

"Are you going to school this morning, Alex?" Robin asked.

"Sure thing. I made my appointment with Mr. Pearson at noon. But I won't have time to come home and change clothes and I want to look my best."

She kissed him.

"I'll be praying for you, Alex."

"Thanks."

He could scarcely wait for school to be dismissed

at noon. While the other kids were filing into the lunchroom to eat, or going home, he drove out to the Highway Service Station.

The Smiths had been trading at the Pearson station since they moved to town and Alex knew the bald, thin-faced station owner well. Yet his heart was pounding as he pulled up at the pumps and stopped.

Mr. Pearson came out.

"Hello, Alex."

"Hi."

"Want some gas?"

He shook his head. His mouth was dry and cottony and his forehead moist.

"I–I came to talk to you about – you know – I called you last night."

Mr. Pearson eyed him owlishly.

"Better move your car," he rasped. "Somebody might want gas while we're talkin'."

Alex pulled up a few feet, backed the car out of the way, and got out. Mr. Pearson looked him over.

"Your dad says you want a job pretty bad."

"I sure do." His voice raised. "I'll do anything, Mr. Pearson. I don't care what it is. I've just got to have a job."

"So, you'll do anything," the station owner repeated. "Does that mean you'll even work a little?"

"Just try me and you'll see."

"What makes you think you can handle a job like this?" He shot the question at Alex without warning.

"I–I don't know," the boy stammered. "I've always liked to fool around with cars, and I've helped take care of Dad's, and–."

Mr. Pearson nodded, his face expressionless. There was no way for Alex to know whether he was making a good impression or not.

"You were quite a football player last year, weren't you?"

"I–I guess I did all right."

"What about your grades?"

"I've been getting by."

"I'm not interested in a kid who's just getting by," Pearson retorted, eyes squinting. "I'm not interested in a guy who's only concerned about football and basketball. I want somebody who can think. Somebody who'll be able to satisfy my customers and bring new ones in."

"Just try me, Mr. Pearson," Alex pleaded. "That's all I ask you. Give me a chance. "I'll show you that I can take care of this job better than anybody else you've ever had on it."

The station owner pulled in a deep breath.

"I suppose you've got some references I can check out? Some teachers at school who know you well enough to tell me whether you're honest or will steal me blind."

Hurriedly Alex gave him the names of two teachers and a couple of business friends of his dad's. Mr. Pearson wrote them on a piece of greasy paper with a pencil stub.

"Thanks for coming out, Alex."

The boy shifted from one foot to the other, uneasily.

"Wh-when will you know whether you want me or not?" he asked.

Pearson screwed his mouth thoughtfully.

"I don't know. I s'pose I could check out these references this afternoon. Why don't you give me your phone number? I'll call you tonight and let you know whether I can use you or not."

"We don't have a telephone, Mr. Pearson. Would it be all right if I call you at about seven-thirty?"

The older man pursed his lips.

"Better make it about eight o'clock if you're going to call me, Alex. That'll give me a little more time."

"Thanks!" The boy's eyes brightened noticeably. "Thanks a lot."

He started for the door and was almost outside when he stopped and turned back.

"!'m sorry, Mr. Pearson, but I almost forgot to ask you about the hours I'd be working. When would you want me to start in the mornings?"

"Same as the other guy. Seven in the morning until six at night, Monday through Friday. And, of course, you'd have to take your turn working extra hours on the weekends."

Alex's smile faded.

"But–."

The station owner saw the change in his face.

"What's the matter, Alex?" he demanded pointedly. "Did you decide you don't want the job, after all?"

"It's not that, at all. I sure do want the job." The boy breathed deeply. "I want it more than I've ever wanted anything in my whole life, but I–I don't know whether I can take it or not."

"And why can't you take it?" Mr. Pearson demanded testily. "The hours too long for you? This ain't a banker's job, you know. We're runnin' a filling station."

"I–I haven't graduated from high school yet," the boy said, "and I was trying to figure out how I'd be able to work it."

The service station owner shrugged his shoulders.

"What you do or don't do about school ain't nothin' to me. But I can tell you when I've got to have a man. If I do decide you're the best man for the job, you'll have to work when I can use you. That's the hours I said. You'll have to take it or leave it."

Nervously the boy shifted from one foot to the other.

"Well, how about it?" the man continued. "Do you want to be considered for the job, or don't you? If you don't, there's no use in wastin' your time and mine."

"Oh, sure," Alex told him. "I want to be considered for the job. Sure I do. Only–." His voice trailed miserably away.

"OK. I'll be gettin' in touch with you."

CHAPTER 2

MR. EVANS' BAD NEWS

Alex got into the car and started the engine. This was something he hadn't counted on. He had always planned on graduating from high school. In fact, he had thought it would be good to go on and get his college degree. There was so little time left. He couldn't quit now.

But he and Robin had been counting so strongly on that job. What would she say when she found out he couldn't take it? What would she think?

Bitterness clouded his eyes. That Pearson character could let him work around his school hours if he wanted to. He could plan something so he could be in school until the end of the school term. He just wanted to be contrary.

Alex drove Robin's red convertible into the school parking lot and got out. She would be waiting for him at the front door, out of breath and fluttery, talking about how she had been praying for him!

A lot of good that had done! If he got the job, he'd have to quit school to take it. That was a fine deal!

He paused for a moment. If he did what he felt like, he wouldn't even go to school that afternoon. But if he didn't, Robin would probably give him fits for it, and especially for running off with her car. She thought more of that stupid car than she did of him.

Alex had been right about one thing. Robin was waiting for him near the front door of the school building. As he came up the walk, she ran out to meet him.

"Oh, Alex," she exclaimed breathlessly, "did you get to see Mr. Pearson?"

"I saw him."

"How did you make out?"

Alex shrugged his shoulders.

"What happened, Alex? Tell me."

His eyes reflected his concern.

"I don't know yet," he said, keeping his voice down so the kids who were going by wouldn't hear him. "But to be blunt about it, I don't know if I'll be able to take it, even if I do get it."

"Why not?" she asked pointedly.

"He wants someone to work full time. That's why not. If I go to work out at the service station, I'll have to quit school."

"Oh–." The color drained from her cheeks.

"Oh, Alex! That would be terrible. You've got to stay in school and graduate. I wouldn't want that, at all. Even if you *never* got a job."

He squinted at her.

It was good to hear her talk that way. A lot of girls would blow up a storm over a husband who was going to school and didn't have a job. Robin was different than most girls. She really had sense.

"It's just my luck," he complained bitterly. "I hunt for a job for weeks without any success. Then I do find one I've got a chance of getting, and it's a job I'll have to quit school for."

"There'll be other jobs," she said with confidence that seemed to lend strength to him.

"I wonder."

"We're not going to worry about it," she told him firmly. "And we're not going to let it interfere with your education. I don't care how badly we need money. You're too close to getting your diploma to quit school now – not even for the best job in town."

They walked up the steps and into the school.

"It sure helps to have you feel that way, Robin." The strength went out of his voice. "But right now, I feel like checking out of here and going straight to work. You're my wife. I'm tired of having your parents and mine support you."

"It won't be for long."

"It's been too long already."

"But Alex, you're almost out of school!" she exclaimed, grasping his arm. "You've got to get your diploma. You've just got to!"

Their eyes met.

"We'll talk about it later."

"There's nothing to talk about," she retorted. "You'll leave school when we graduate and not a day before."

He smiled down at her.

"I don't know how I'd ever get along without you, Robin," he said warmly. "These past few months have been so tough I don't think I'd have been able to take it if you weren't standing by me.

A warm glow enveloped her. That was almost better than having Alex get the job – knowing that he felt that way about her. It was wonderful to have him say that he needed her – that she was a help to him. That was the way it was always going to be for the rest of their lives. They were going to stand together, regardless of what happened.

That afternoon Alex was waiting for Robin on the front steps when school was out.

"Going to be using your car this afternoon?" he asked her.

"Our car," she corrected.

He grinned down at her.

"Are you going to be using it?"

"I thought I'd go over and see Mother for a while," she said.

"That's OK. I can walk."

"What were you going to do?"

"I thought I'd go out and see if I can find a part-time job – anything to get us a little money until I can get out of school."

"I can go home any time, Alex. You take the car. You need it more than I do."

Alex offered to take Robin over to her mother's, but she decided to go home.

"I've got some things to do," she said.

"I'll be back as soon as I can."

Her smile was warm and reassuring.

"I just know you're going to find work today, Alex," she said.

He wished he could be as sure of it as she was. In spite of himself, he was as discouraged and dejected as he had ever been since they were married. And the places he stopped to ask for work did nothing to dispel his gloom.

"Sorry, Alex," the supermarket manager said, "but I've got more part-time help than I need right now.

I've been thinking of laying off one of the boys because I don't have enough work for him."

"If I needed anyone," an uptown service station owner told him, "it would be full time. It's too hard to work around school hours or another job. Just the time we'd need a man the most, he'd have to be off."

It was that way wherever he went. There wasn't any work for him.

Alex drove around town slowly, unable to bring himself to go back to the apartment and see Robin again. It was tough for her having a husband who couldn't get a job – who couldn't even earn the money to support her, he thought.

He felt like quitting school and taking a full-time job. That's what he felt like doing.

For a moment, his temper flared. The business-men around Fairview expected guys to stay in town after they got out of high school and were married, but they wouldn't hire them. It was their own fault if most of the kids moved away as fast as they could.

That's what he was going to do. He'd shake the dust of the place from his feet but good, just as soon as he got his diploma. He and Robin would pull stakes and go to Minneapolis, Duluth, or somewhere like that. Then maybe some of those characters would wish they had given him a job.

He pulled up before the dilapidated apartment house and for a time sat in the car. He even hated to go into that dump.

He should take that job at Highway Service, even if he did have to quit school to do it. A guy wouldn't have to have his high school diploma to run a service station. That was for sure. He could handle one if Mr. Pearson could.

If he took the job, he could get Robin out of that crummy upstairs apartment and into a decent place.

But every time he thought about quitting school something inside him died. He hadn't actually known how badly he wanted his diploma until now.

Finally, he went upstairs to their apartment.

"Robin, I'm home," he called as he opened the door.

No answer.

Her dad was sitting in the living room, his face taut and drawn. Usually, his eyes danced and he was smiling, but not today.

"Hi."

"Hello, Alex."

Robin was sitting across from her dad, her pretty young face ashen and her lips trembling.

Slowly the boy crossed the room and sat down in a creaky chair near the window.

"I didn't expect to see you here this afternoon," he said.

"I didn't expect to be here." Mr. Evans moistened his lips with the tip of his tongue. "But I have something I have to talk to you about and I thought it would be best to get you together."

"Yes?"

Concern stood full in Robin's eyes, and he thought he saw tears lurking just beneath her eyelids.

"Daddy has some bad news for us, Alex," Robin said. "He hasn't told me what it is yet."

Alex stared at him quizzically.

"It can't be any worse than the news I've been getting all afternoon trying to find work."

"I want you both to know that this isn't anything I have wanted to do. In fact, both Mother and I have held off on it as long as we could."

"What are you talking about, Daddy?" Robin broke in. "Don't keep us in suspense like this."

"I told you after you got married that I had been

having some rather severe financial reverses," he said. "Remember?"

They both nodded.

"We were getting behind before, but after you got married the extra load put us in a tight squeeze."

"Alex has been trying to do something about that, Daddy," Robin said. "He's been out this afternoon trying to find work."

"It's just until school's out, Mr. Evans. Then I'm going to get a job and take care of Robin myself." His face muscles tightened. "Believe me, it's harder for me to have to take money from you and my parents than it is for you to have to give it."

"I appreciate that."

"If we have to, we'll go to Minneapolis or Duluth or somewhere else to find work."

Mr. Evans acted as though he scarcely heard him.

"I know you want to do your part toward supporting Robin, but my problem is immediate. I've got to do something to lighten the load I'm carrying."

"What do you mean?" Alex asked.

"I know." Tears trembled in Robin's eyes. "What Daddy's trying to say is that he's taking my car and– and selling it."

CHAPTER 3

ALEX – HIGH SCHOOL DROPOUT

Alex stared at Mr. Evans in growing bewilderment. His eyelids opened wide and his lower jaw sagged.

"But–but–," he began, lamely seeking for words.

Mr. Evans took a pencil from his pocket and fingered it uneasily.

"I think Mother and I feel much worse about this than either of you do," he said. "I'd rather do almost anything else than take your car, because I know how much it means to you."

"Couldn't we try to work out something so–so Alex and I could take over the payments?" Robin asked numbly.

"I don't see how you could do that. Alex isn't even able to pay your grocery bill."

Alex flinched.

"The point is, I've got a chance to sell the car now and get back some of the money we've already put into it, in addition to cutting down on the payments. So, it will help us in two ways."

Robin's lips trembled.

"But Daddy!" she cried. The old accusing tone came back into her voice. "You can't take the car away from me! You gave it to me. It's mine!"

"I know. That's why I feel so bad about taking the car away from you. But we have no other choice. Believe me."

"It isn't fair," she retorted. "It isn't fair at all!"

There was a tense silence.

"I don't know why you gave it to me, if you thought you'd have to take it back."

"Robin," he said sternly, "I don't want to remind you of this. I've been trying to avoid saying anything that would hurt you any more than you're already being hurt. But you are directly responsible for our having to take the car away from you. Don't forget that."

"What do you mean?" she demanded.

"It was your marriage and the extra obligations we had to assume in helping you that's making this necessary. If it wasn't for that, we wouldn't be doing what we're doing now."

Tears came to her eyes.

"If you're going to take it away from us I–I suppose there's nothing we can say or do about it. We–we'll bring it over tomorrow afternoon when school's out. Will that be all right?"

He shook his head.

"I'm sorry, Robin, but it won't. I've got to take the car over to the garage tonight. They called me earlier this afternoon and told me they would have to have it tonight. They've sold it already and want to get it cleaned up and ready for delivery tomorrow."

"Wh–who bought it?"

"I don't know for sure." His throat choked on the words. "I think the father of one of the girls who's graduating this spring is buying it for a graduation gift."

Robin's temper flared.

"No!" she exclaimed. "You can't do that to me! You wouldn't!"

"I didn't have any choice in the matter. When I told the garage I wanted to sell the car I couldn't place any restrictions on them."

"You mean you sold it before you even came and talked to me about it?" she demanded. "You didn't tell me first?"

"I've tried to explain to you!"

She got to her feet, stomped over to the table and picked up the car keys Alex had laid down moments before. When she spoke once more her voice was frigid.

"Here are the keys, Daddy," she said. "Now, I hope you're satisfied!"

He took the keys and put them in his pocket.

"All the kids in school will know what happened. They all know my car. I–I'll never be able to hold my head up again!"

"I–I'm sorry, Robin!"

"You're sorry! A lot of good that's going to do. You've already sold the car."

Her dad started to reply but checked himself. Without a word he left the apartment and walked slowly down the steep stairs. Alex stood motionless near the door, his gaze riveted on his young wife.

"Robin," he said softly.

No answer.

"Robin."

Still, she did not speak.

"Robin," he repeated once more. "I'm sorry you aren't going to be able to keep your car. Honest, I am."

Her eyes flashed fire from her ashen face.

"You *should* be sorry I'm not going to get to keep it!" she almost screamed. "If you'd gotten a job when we first got married like most men this wouldn't have happened."

"You know I tried."

"A lot of good it did, too! Nobody would hire you!" Tears streamed down her face. "If you'd been working, we'd have been able to keep the car! It's all your fault!"

Her words slammed the breath from Alex and his face paled. He took half a step backwards, involuntarily, as though she had hit him. His temper flared to match hers.

"If you're so anxious to have me get a job," he cried, "OK, I'll get a job!"

She laughed derisively.

"You get a job?" she echoed. "That's a good one! You won't even try to find work as long as Daddy's paying all our bills for us."

"He's not paying all of them. My dad's paying half, you know!"

The silence between them was deafening.

"Or had you forgotten that?" he asked, his lips curling bitterly.

"I wouldn't brag about it, if I were you," she continued. "Most married men don't have to depend on their parents for support. They go out and get jobs and support themselves."

Angrily Alex stared into her blazing eyes; then he turned and started for the door. As he moved to go, Robin softened slightly. She pivoted in his direction.

"Alex," she said weakly.

He opened the door and for a moment or two stood there uncertainly.

"Alex?" Her voice rose.

He whirled about.

"Now what do you want?"

As she looked at him, her anger seeped away. The hurt was deep in his eyes. She had never seen such anguish on his face.

"You aren't going to leave, are you?"

"What's it to you, if I do?"

"Please don't."

She moved toward him, but he stepped out onto the little porch.

"I'll be back after 'while," he said, testily.

"Where are you going?"

"Out!"

"Alex!" she exclaimed. "Please don't go. I didn't mean what I said, honestly, I didn't. I know you've tried to get a job and all that. I just–." Her voice trailed away as she realized he was already storming down the stairs.

Robin remained motionless in the middle of the floor for a moment or two. Then she half-stumbled across the room and sank into the nearest chair.

Why did she have to talk to him that way? The things she said weren't true. She had only said them because she was hurt and angry at her dad.

She straightened slowly, listening.

Was that Alex on the stairs? He'd be coming back before long. He wouldn't leave her this way. He loved her too much for that. He'd start thinking about the terrible things he had said to her and would stop before he reached the bottom of the stairs. He would stand there a couple of minutes or so wrestling with his conscience. Then he'd come sheepishly back and tell her how sorry he was for getting mad at her. She'd tell him how sorry she was, too, and it would all be over.

Robin hunched down in the chair again and dabbed at her eyes.

She really didn't care so much about losing the car, although it was going to be hard going to school and seeing someone else driving it. What really mattered was Alex. She couldn't let the car cause any trouble between them, regardless of what else happened.

They could walk for a few weeks or months. When they got out of high school Alex would be able to get a good job. They'd soon have a good car again – and maybe even a new little home. Then all of this would seem so petty and insignificant. They'd probably both be laughing about it.

She went to the bathroom, washed her face in cold water, and combed her hair. She wanted to be looking nice when Alex came back.

But fifteen minutes or more passed before she heard his footsteps on the stairs. He wasn't coming up hesitantly, as he usually did after they had quarreled. This time his steps were heavy and measured. Determined was the word for them. He flung the door open decisively and she came hurriedly into the other room.

"Alex?" she called.

He did not answer, but his footsteps on the kitchen floor gave him away. She ran to the door.

"Alex!"

He did not speak to her.

"Alex, I–I want to talk to you." Her anger melted. "I–I'm sorry for everything I said, Alex. It–it wasn't very nice of me."

"You should have thought of that before."

"What do you mean?" Fear clutched at her throat.

"Let's go in the living room and sit down. I want to talk to you."

Meekly she did as he said.

He sat across from her, his gaze focusing on her tear-stained face.

"What's the matter, Alex?" she asked.

"I just want to tell you that I did it!" There was triumph in his voice.

"You did what?" she demanded.

"I got the service station job." He paused significantly. "And what's more, Robin, I told Mr. Pearson that I'd take it."

She gasped.

"Oh, Alex! No!"

"That's what you were screaming at me about, isn't it?" he asked angrily. "Isn't that what you've been wanting me to do ever since we got married?"

"I wanted you to get a job," she admitted, "but I didn't–."

"All right! You wanted me to get a job, so I got a job!" He was still furious.

"But what about school, Alex?" she asked plaintively. "What about your high school diploma?"

He shrugged his shoulders.

"Who needs a diploma to peddle gasoline?"

"But–."

"Besides, I've had my fill of school. And I've had my fill of listening to you hound me about not going to work. So that's what I've done. I've taken a job and I'm going to work. Who needs a high school diploma!

Robin started to cry.

CHAPTER 4

DANNY AND KAY'S CONCERN

Danny and Kay Orlis were driving from the airport to town when they approached the Highway Service Station. Danny slowed down and flicked on his turn signal.

"What are you stopping here for?" Kay asked.

He laughed.

"Our car needs gas every once in a while," he told her. "Or weren't you aware of that?"

"Smarty."

Alex came out to wait on them. He stopped suddenly, halfway to the car, his face flushing as he saw who it was. For an instant he seemed undecided whether to go on to the car or turn back to the building.

"Hello, Alex."

When Danny spoke to him, he grinned self-consciously and approached the car window.

"Hello, Mr. Orlis. How're you?"

"Fine, thank you."

"Fill 'er up?"

Danny nodded.

As Alex moved to the back of the car Danny got out and joined him.

"Alex, I didn't know you were working here."

"I haven't been working here very long," he answered. "To tell you the truth, I just started here this morning."

The youthful missionary waited in silence while Alex filled the car with gas and opened the hood to check the oil and water.

"Something special going on that they let school out today?" Danny asked.

"Nope." The Smith boy's mouth tightened firmly. "I'm just not going to school anymore. That's all. I quit and came to work here."

Danny stared at him incredulously.

"You're not going to school anymore?" he echoed.

"That's right."

"You must be joking."

By this time Alex' handsome face flushed scarlet.

"Nope, I'm not joking. I just decided to quit goofing off. So, I quit school and got a job out here to earn a living for Robin and me." His lips quivered slightly. "A guy should earn a living for his wife, shouldn't he?"

Danny did not answer him. In fact, he said no more until Alex had given him his change and they were about to leave.

"Alex," he said abruptly, "we're having Bible club

at our house tonight. How about bringing Robin and coming over?"

"Nope!" he retorted, eyes snapping. "I don't want anything to do with that stuff. Robin's got enough religion for both of us."

Danny did not press him. There was no use in talking to Alex while he was in that mood.

"If you change your mind," Danny went on, "we'd like to have you."

"Don't count on it."

The young missionary got his change and drove thoughtfully away from the station.

"Did you know Alex had quit school, Kay?" he asked.

She shook her head.

"Not until right now. I was as surprised as you were."

"I wish I could have talked with him before he quit. It's such a short time until graduation."

"It sounded to me as though he had his mind pretty well made up."

"You can say that again."

Danny pulled into their driveway and stopped.

"Danny, do you think it would do any good if I were to go over and talk with Robin tomorrow?" Kay asked as they were getting out of the car.

"About what?"

"I don't know that it would be about anything special. Coming to Bible club, I guess. I was thinking that she probably needs a very good friend right now. Someone she trusts and can confide in."

"It certainly wouldn't hurt to make yourself available in case she does need counseling."

Kay walked into the house in silence and took off her coat.

"You'll be praying about it, won't you, Danny?" she asked.

That night they had a special time of prayer for Robin and Alex, and the next afternoon Kay went over to their apartment. Robin was there alone.

"Kay!" she exclaimed, her voice brightening as she saw who was at the door. "I'm so glad to see you. Come on in."

"How are you, Robin?"

"All right, I guess." The youthful bride fought a smile into place and held it there forcibly. "This is the first time you've been over to see us since–since we've been married."

"That's right, and I'm ashamed of myself for it." Kay looked around, smiling. "My, you have a nice little apartment."

In spite of her efforts, the smile faded from Robin's lips.

"It's not as nice as we'd like to have it," she replied, "but it's all we can afford right now."

"I think it's very nice."

Kay sat down in an easy chair and for several minutes they talked about many things. Robin asked about Bible club, who was coming and whether any of the kids were showing concern for spiritual things.

"Not as much as we'd like," Kay replied.

Robin hesitated.

"You know, Kay," she said suddenly, "when I get to thinking about Bible club, I get so lonesome for it I can hardly stand it."

"That's very interesting," the older girl said. "That's one of the reasons I stopped by this afternoon."

"It is?" Robin regarded her intently.

"I thought I'd stop by and see if you and Alex would like to come tonight."

Hopelessness tinged the girl's voice. "I'd like to come, Kay. Honestly, I would. Like I said, you don't know how much I miss Bible club. But Alex has to work tonight."

"That's too bad."

"If it wasn't for that, I'd love to come."

"If he's going to be working, maybe you'd like to come yourself. Would you like to have me stop by and pick you up?"

Robin paused.

"I'd really like that, but I–I don't think I'd better. Not with things like they are right now."

She acted as though she had more to tell Kay, and the older girl waited patiently.

"Alex is a wonderful guy," she went on at last, defensively. "There isn't anyone better in the whole world and I love him more than I ever thought I'd be able to love anyone."

Kay smiled understandingly.

But he–he doesn't like Bible Club or–or things like that and doesn't want me to get too involved in them. So, for a while I think I'd better not come."

"I see." Kay did not press the matter further. She changed the subject then. It was not until she got up to go that she mentioned it again.

"If you don't feel that you can come over to club tonight, would it be all right if I came over to see you while Danny has it?"

"Well–." Robin gazed at her uneasily.

"It's been such a long time since we've had a chance to visit."

"I–I suppose it would be all right for you to come, if you want to." She caught herself. "I don't mean that the way it sounds, Kay. I want you to come. In fact, I'd love to have you. But I–I hate to have you miss club yourself."

"I think it would be all right if I miss it tonight. I'll be over about eight this evening."

Alex came home for supper that night at about six. Robin was sitting in the living room trying to read a magazine. She looked up as he entered. Her lips trembled as she started to speak.

"H-hello, Alex."

He stopped in the doorway, studying her serious young face.

"Hello, Robin."

"Supper will be ready in a few minutes. I have it in the oven." Hurt still edged her voice and dulled the laughter in her eyes.

"That's all right. I'm not very hungry."

She looked down at the magazine, but the words swam before her eyes. Alex still had not moved. He was looking at her in the same quizzical way.

"Robin," he said at last, voice choking, "I–I've got to talk to you."

She put the magazine aside.

"Yes?"

He came over and sat down beside her.

"I–I'm sorry about getting mad and lipping off to you the way I did and–and everything," he blurted. "I didn't mean it."

Her slender body stiffened.

"If you didn't mean it, you shouldn't have said it."

"I–I guess I was just mad and hurt because of the thing you said to me. I've felt awful since–since the other night."

Tears quivered on her eyelids.

"So–so have I,'" she stammered.

Silence hung heavily between them.

"I–I'm sorry for the things I said to you, too, Alex," she admitted. "I should never have talked to you the way I did. I knew you had been trying as hard as you could to get a job. I–I was just mad and hurt because I had to give up the car, so I tried to lay the blame on you. I–I've been miserable the last two days."

He put his arm around her and drew her close to him. For the space of a minute or two they clung to each other.

"We're never going to let this happen again," he said firmly. "I don't care what happens. You and I are not going to have any more fights. And that's a promise. I don't care what happens."

She continued to cry for a time, quietly. It was a while before either of them spoke.

"You don't know how badly I feel that you quit school, Alex," she said at last. "I–I wanted you to graduate."

His face grew hard. For an instant, his lips quivered.

"I don't want to quit, either," he answered truthfully. "To be honest with you, I've been thinking about it all day."

Her face brightened.

"Then why don't you go back to the school and tell them you want to stay and graduate."

"I can't," he said miserably. "I already promised Mr. Pearson that I'd work for him. It's too late now."

She sat up straight.

"I don't see why. You could go to Mr. Pearson tonight and tell him that you've changed your mind. Tell him you realize how foolish it is for you to leave school now when it's so close to graduation. He'll understand. He might even let you keep your job there or hire you again after school is out. You said he liked the way you work."

Alex got to his feet and paced slowly across the room to sit in a chair near the door. His smooth young face was deeply lined.

"It's not only Mr. Pearson," he said. "I went down to school yesterday morning and checked out. They tried to talk me into staying and I–I sort of lost my temper and lipped off to them. They wouldn't let me back again, even if I tried."

"Oh, Alex."

She started to cry again.

He went back over to her and put his arm clumsily about her shoulders.

"Now, Robin," he began, "that isn't going to do any good. We've got to go on from here."

"B-but now you won't be able to graduate with me," she said.

He started to speak but checked himself and looked quickly away to hide the hurt in his eyes. It was a long while before he said anything at all. When he did, his voice rang with confidence.

"Maybe I won't graduate this semester," he said with new determination. "But I'll work hard this summer and we'll save every penny we can. Then next September I'll go back to school."

Robin smiled timidly.

"Do–do you think you could?"

"Sure I can." The very words seemed to give him new confidence. "We'll get a little money squirreled away and I'll go back and stay until I graduate. You wait and see."

Her smile spread.

"Oh, Alex, you don't know how happy it would make me if I knew you were really going to go back and get your diploma. You will promise me, won't you?"

"That's one promise I don't even have to think about before I make. You can bet I'll go back to school. I want to graduate even worse than you want me to."

She threw her arms around him and kissed him impulsively.

"You're not mad at me anymore?" he asked.

"Mad at you? How could I be?"

CHAPTER 5

SOME HELPFUL ADVICE

Alex had to work at the station that evening and only had an hour off for supper. They talked so long he almost missed getting something to eat. Robin looked at her watch.

"Oh, Alex," she exclaimed, "look what time it is, and we haven't eaten yet."

"I can grab a sandwich and eat it on the way."

"I don't want you to do that," she said disappointedly. "I fixed some things in the oven that I–I thought you would like."

"OK." He went into the kitchen and started pulling dishes from the cupboard. "I'll help you set the table. You put the food on. We'll eat in a hurry."

He wolfed his meal and pushed his chair back from the table.

"Sorry I've got to run, Robin, but Mr. Pearson's a bear about being late. And he's staying at the station himself until I get back."

He bent and kissed her goodbye.

"That was a super meal."

She smiled up at him. "What time will you be home tonight, Alex?"

"I don't know for sure. It depends on what time I can get away from the station."

He saw the sorrow and concern in her eyes.

"I should be back about ten, I suppose. It won't be long after that."

"Come as soon as you can."

For a long while after he was gone, she sat in the living room staring at the floor. Everything might work out all right, after all. If Alex would go back to high school and get his diploma things would be different for them. Then perhaps he could go on to college and get his degree and he'd be on the same footing with the other guys in his class.

It was because of her that he wasn't going to get to graduate this spring. If he didn't have her to support, he'd have been able to stay in school and get his diploma when the rest of the class got theirs. And he'd have gone on to college, too. Probably on a football scholarship. He might even have gotten to play professional football. Some of the people around town had been talking that way during the football season.

If she just hadn't exploded when her dad told them about taking the car back, Alex would still be in school. If he didn't get his diploma, it was all her fault. Tears came to her eyes again. She was costing Alex an awful lot.

Then she remembered that Kay was coming over to spend the evening. Sighing deeply, she went into the kitchen and started to wash the dishes. She was just clearing the table when there was a knock at the door. She went to answer it.

"Hello, Robin," Kay said brightly.

"Oh, hello." She was so flustered that it was a moment before she invited her guest in. "I–I didn't expect you quite so soon."

"I thought it would be a bit easier for me to leave if I got away from the house before the kids started to come."

Robin managed a thin laugh.

"I was just sitting in the living room," she admitted. "I knew you were coming, but I couldn't bring myself to get out here and start washing dishes. I fooled around longer than I should have."

"I know just what you mean. I do that myself once in a while."

There was a short pause.

"Before I got married," the younger girl said, "I had no idea how much work is involved in keeping house. It seems as though I never get finished. By the time I've got one job done there are three others waiting to be taken care of."

Kay took off her sweater and Robin took it into the bedroom and put it on the bed.

"Why don't we do the dishes together?" Kay suggested. "We can talk at the same time."

Robin felt the color creep up into her cheeks.

"I can take care of them later."

"I'd like to help you."

"It makes me feel foolish having you come over and help me with my work. You have your own home to keep up."

"Don't feel so badly," Kay said, laughing good-naturedly. "I stacked our dishes this evening."

The younger girl gasped.

"You did?"

"You're not the only one who gets behind once in a while." She took a dish towel off the rack and approached the sink. "And I'll tell you something else. If anyone comes to my house and offers to help with the dishes, they get a job. I'm not bashful about letting them."

They set to work.

"Tonight I had an excuse for leaving the dishes," Kay went on, "or at least I thought I did. Danny wanted to go over to the parsonage and talk to Pastor Reeves about something that had to do with Young People's, and I had some things to finish before the kids came to club, so the dishes were left tonight."

"Alex and I got to talking tonight," Robin said, "and–and–." Her voice trailed away miserably.

Kay caught the hurt in Robin's voice but did not mention it until Robin brought up the subject.

"You knew Alex quit school, didn't you?"

"Danny and I stopped in at the station for gas and saw him there. We were sorry to hear it."

"Did he tell you why he quit?"

"He just said he'd quit, that's all."

Robin turned back to the sink, looking down to keep Kay from reading the anguish in her eyes.

"How have things been going between you and Alex?" Kay asked gently.

Robin finished washing the last of the dishes, wiped off the table and stove, and drained the water from the sink.

"All right, I guess," she answered at last.

Kay squinted.

"You don't sound very sure," she said.

Robin glanced her way quickly, before averting her gaze once more.

"Everything's all right, Kay," she said. "Really it is.

"I'm glad of that, Robin." Kay shook out the dish towel and hung it on the rack to dry. "Somehow Danny and I had the idea that you two were finding the road a little rocky right now."

"I–," the young bride swallowed hard. "I–that is–." Tears came up in her eyes and trembled there. "I'm sorry I told you that everything's all right, Kay. I–I didn't mean to tell you something that isn't true." Now that she had started, the words came out with a rush.

"You don't have to tell me anything, Robin," the older girl replied quietly. "But if you think it would help to talk, I'd be glad to listen. Danny and I would like to help you if we can."

Robin's lips twitched nervously.

"You knew there was something wrong, didn't you?"

she asked. "Isn't that the reason you came over to see me tonight instead of staying home for Bible club?"

Kay nodded.

"I didn't plan on prying into your personal affairs. But, as Danny suggested, I just wanted to make myself available in case you had some problems you would like to talk out."

"I suppose you're thinking, 'I told her so! I tried to tell her she shouldn't go steady in high school. I tried to tell her that she shouldn't think about getting married until she got her diploma and went on to school for a while'." Robin's voice rose defensively.

"Now, Robin," Kay replied. There was a note of firmness in her voice that the other girl had never heard before. "I hope you know me better than that. I didn't come over here to gloat or tell you how wrong you've been. I came to help if I can."

The corners of Robin's mouth twitched nervously.

"I'm so mixed up and confused that I don't even know what I'm saying or doing half the time."

"I understand," Kay said, softening. "What's been done has been done and none of us can change it."

The younger girl swallowed against the lump that welled in her throat and her eyes became luminous.

"I–I'm sorry," she stammered. "I didn't mean it the way it sounded."

"Let's go in and sit down." Kay's smile was warm and reassuring. "It might help you a little to unburden yourself of some of the problems you've been facing."

"I–I've been wanting to talk to someone, but I couldn't go to my mother and–and I've been too ashamed to go and talk with you."

"You don't need to feel that way about talking to me. I'm happy to talk to you any time."

"I should have known that. You always have been."

Neither said any more until they were in the living room. Even then Robin hesitated. Kay sat across from her and smiled in encouragement.

"It all started," Robin began, the words coming slowly, "when Daddy came over and told us that I couldn't keep the car – that he was going to have to sell it."

She went on to tell how she had lost her temper and accused Alex, and how they had a terrible quarrel over it.

"So, Alex quit school and took this job," she concluded. "And now things are worse than ever. He won't be able to graduate with us this spring and–and it's all my fault."

"The important thing isn't that you had an argument," Kay said, choosing her words with care. "Or that one or the other of you is at fault. Unfortunately, most young couples and far too many older ones have differences that result in arguments. And usually, one person is more at fault than the other. What really matters is that you get the disagreement straightened out so there isn't any continuing friction between you."

A faint smile tickled the corners of Robin's mouth.

"At least we got our silly argument settled," she said. "We apologized to each other at supper-time tonight. So, we don't have that between us anymore."

"That's fine. When you did that, you took care of the most important problem."

Robin's face clouded.

"But when I get to thinking that Alex isn't going to get his diploma with our class, I feel so badly I don't know what to do."

Kay nodded.

"It would have been a lot better for both you and Alex if he had stayed in school until he got his diploma," she admitted, "but he can go back next semester and finish, if he wants to do it badly enough. This isn't a situation that can't be straightened out."

The hurt still dulled Robin's eyes.

"That will take care of his diploma, all right, but that's only part of what I've been thinking about."

"What do you mean?"

"The rest of the kids he's been going to school with will be gone. They'll be in college or in service or something and–and Alex will still be in high school or working in that filling station."

Kay hesitated. She had to be completely honest with Robin. She couldn't be in the position of telling her something that wasn't true in order to make her feel good. The situation regarding Alex' education was a serious problem for them. She knew from her experience with other kids who had dropped out of high school that he would have problems enough getting his diploma. The chances were that he would never get on to college.

"Danny and I will be much in prayer about it,"

she said. "God can work out all of these things in a very wonderful way."

"Thank you, Kay. You don't know how much better it makes me feel to have someone like you to talk things over with."

For a brief space of time silence hung between them.

"There's something else that bothers me even more than the problem of Alex' education, Robin," Kay continued at last.

"What's that?"

"Danny and I have noticed that you and Alex have only been in Sunday school and church once since you've been married. This is even more serious than the fact that he quit school. You need the church, Robin, if you're going to be a testimony and walk the way God intends a Christian to walk. We all do."

Robin colored delicately and her gaze lowered. When she finally spoke, her voice was dull and lifeless.

"I know," she murmured. "And I think I feel a lot worse about that than I do about anything else. Alex promised me that he would go to Sunday school and church with me after we were married, and I thought sure he would. He seemed so sincere about it. But–," she shrugged helplessly. "He just won't go to church with me. And the more I ask him about it the more determined he seems to be that he isn't going to have anything to do with the things of God." Her lips trembled. "I can't understand it, Kay."

Kay nodded.

"I know just what you mean. I've talked to a number of girls who have had the same problem."

"It's not that Alex isn't a good husband," the young bride said defensively. "He's as good to me as anyone could possibly be. And I do love him, Kay."

'I'm sure you do."

By this time Robin was very close to tears.

"I think loving him the way I do makes it even harder for me. I'm so anxious to have him take Christ as his Savior that I can hardly think of anything else."

Kay smiled.

"God can undertake in this matter, too," she said.

"You've had a lot of experience, Kay," Robin said suddenly. "How can I get Alex to start going to Sunday school and church with me? How can I get him to start listening to the gospel?"

Kay thought carefully before she spoke.

"If I were in your place, Robin," she began, "I believe the very first thing I would do would be to start going to services myself."

"Alone?"

"If I had to go alone, I would. You see, you aren't going to be able to help Alex spiritually if you don't stay close to the Lord yourself."

"I'd never thought of it in quite that way.

"And you'll find it almost impossible to stay close to God unless you are getting strength and help from the ministry of good Sunday school teachers and a godly pastor."

Nervously, Robin got to her feet.

"I've wanted to go to church and Sunday school, but I've been afraid that Alex would never start going with me if I made a practice of going alone."

"I think just the opposite is true," Kay said. "I believe Alex will admire you for it. He may not say anything, but he can't help noting that you are faithful to God. You'll be demonstrating to him that your faith does mean something to you." She paused significantly. "It's all right to ask Alex to go with you occasionally. In fact, I'd advise you to do so once in a while, but you must be very careful not to nag him. That will only make matters worse for both of you. He might get to the place where he stays home just because you want him to go."

"I know what you mean," the other girl answered. "I've made Alex mad at me a couple of times by insisting and insisting that he go to church or some other place with me. Then he just plain won't go."

"That's right. He wants to show you he doesn't have to do what you ask him to. The most important thing for you, or any other girl with a problem like yours, is to pray for him and trust God to work it out."

Robin's eyes gleamed.

"Oh, I do pray for Alex," she exclaimed. "I pray for him every single night."

"Danny and I are praying for him, too, Robin." The girl's eyes lit.

CHAPTER 6

"NEVER A CROSS WORD"

The next evening Alex did not have to work at the filling station. Robin had finished her studies for the next day, and they were home alone.

Alex finished changing his clothes and came into the living room and picked up a magazine.

"I sure wish there was something to do tonight," he said.

She looked up.

"Like what?"

"I don't know." He went over and sat down. "Would you feel like going somewhere?"

"That might be fun. Where do you want to go? Over to see your parents?"

He shook his head.

"I thought about that, but they'll just be sitting around watching television. I'd like to get out with some kids our own age for a change. How about it?"

Robin colored.

"You–you weren't thinking of going to a show or–or something like that, were you?"

Alex squinted at her.

"What if I was?"

"Were you?"

"No, I was thinking about going over and seeing Joe and Nellie this afternoon. They've been after us to go over and see them, but we've never done it."

Robin smiled.

"I think that would be nice."

"But what was that about this 'show' bit?" he continued. "Were you going to give me static if I'd wanted to take in a show?"

"I misunderstood you, Alex," she said, "that's all." She got up and started for the bedroom. "I'll be ready as soon as I get my clothes changed."

"You don't have to dress up for them."

"I know I don't, but Nellie always looks so nice when I've seen her," Robin protested. "I wouldn't think of going over to visit them without changing clothes. It won't take a minute."

As soon as she was ready, they left the house and walked across town to the apartment building where their married friends lived.

"If we had your car, we could take them for a ride," Alex said.

"I'd just as soon sit in their apartment and visit or play Monopoly or Scrabble."

They walked on for half a block.

"It's times like these when I really miss that car of yours," he told her. "If we had it this evening, we'd be over there by this time."

"We'll get along," she told him firmly. "A lot of kids get by without a car when they're first married. We can manage."

"Sure we can." He glanced at her from the corner of his eyes. "But it still would be nice to have a car. Any kind of an old car."

Robin made no comment.

"I got to thinking about that this afternoon at the station. A lot of guys come around with old cars they want to sell. Maybe we could buy one on payments. It wouldn't have to be much. Just something that would get us around until we can afford a good car."

She stopped and turned to face him.

"I think I'd like to have a car just as much as you would, Alex."

"Then it's all settled." His face brightened. "We'll start looking around the first thing in the morning."

"That's not what I was going to say. If we got a car we'd have payments and insurance and gas and oil and maybe have to get it fixed once in a while. We've got more important things to think about than a car."

"Like what?" he asked testily.

"We've got to get ourselves situated so you can go back and finish school."

His face hardened and he did not speak immediately.

"And going on to college," she added. "That's important, too. When you get your college degree, we can think about getting a car."

His voice grew cold.

"Let's get my high school diploma before we start thinking about my going on to college, OK? Right now, I don't know whether I'll ever get either one."

"Oh, you will," she said, confidence and hope mingling in her voice. "As soon as school is out, I'm going to get a job. I'll save my money and put it in the bank so we can have it when you go to school."

"And just what kind of a job could *you* get?" he demanded. "Would you want to do housework or be a waitress in a cafe?"

She hesitated. That was something she had not thought about until that very moment. But what Alex said was true. She wasn't trained for much of anything. She had taken an academic course in high school to prepare herself for college. She could type, but she made a lot of mistakes and wasn't fast enough to get a job that required typing. And she had never taken book-keeping or shorthand. She did want to work, but what sort of work was there that she would be able to do?

"I–I don't know what kind of a job I could get, Alex," she replied, "but I–I'm going to try to get something."

They started up the stairs to their friends' apartment. The window was open and they could hear Nellie and Joe plainly.

"Nellie!"

"Don't shout at me!"

"I'll shout at you if I want to!" Anger coarsened his voice. "What I want to know is when are you going to clean up this filthy hole?"

"I'll clean it when I get good and ready. Is that answer enough for you?"

"The whole sink's full of dirty dishes and I haven't had a clean shirt for two days."

Nellie's voice was shrill with anger.

"When am I going to clean up this hole?" she echoed. "You're a good one to ask me that. Just whose stuff is scattered around the place, anyway? Answer me that!"

"It's a woman's job to keep the house clean."

He paused and they could hear his footsteps as he walked from one room to the other.

"Just look at it! If this was a pigpen even the pigs wouldn't be able to stand it. They'd move out!"

Silence.

"If I didn't have to work all day and help support myself, I could keep the house clean," Nellie retorted. "But I've got to work and keep up the house, too. If I didn't, we'd starve to death. We couldn't live on what you make."

Robin turned to Alex.

"Oh, Alex!" she said under her breath. "Let's leave."

"I think we'd better."

The steps creaked under his feet.

Inside, Joe swore at his wife savagely.

"Shut your big mouth and go answer the door! We've got company."

"Go answer it yourself. I'm just a slave around here. I've got to get to work. It's not enough that I've been working as many hours today as you have."

In the pause that followed, Alex and Robin stared helplessly at each other.

"What'll we do now, Alex?" she asked. "They know we're here."

Before he could answer, the door opened and they saw Joe standing there. He was still in his greasy work clothes, except for his shoes. He had taken them off and held one in his hand. His face stained crimson and he managed an embarrassed laugh.

"Hi."

"W-we were just going by," Alex said apologetically, "and–and thought maybe we would stop by and see you for a few minutes. But–."

"We weren't expecting any company tonight," Joe stammered. "I–I mean–." He turned his head and called over his shoulder, "Nellie, guess what? Alex and Robin are here. They've come over to see us."

There was no sound from within the apartment.

"I–I think we'd better go," Robin said, taking half a step away from the door. "We'll come back some other evening when we have more time."

"Don't rush off before Nellie gets here," Joe protested. "She'll never forgive me if I let you leave before she gets here to say 'hi' to you."

Joe did not ask them to come in. Instead, he kept them on the steps talking with them. After a long while Nellie joined him. She was dressed in a faded duster and her uncombed hair straggled about her tear-streaked face. She, too, flushed crimson.

"I–I'm so sorry we can't ask you in," she said. "but we–we were just getting ready to go out for the evening, weren't we, Darling?"

Joe eyed her questioningly.

"Oh," he said. "Oh, yeah. We–we're going out tonight. Why don't you come back and see us again soon – like tomorrow evening?"

"Do that," Nellie put in quickly.

"Come over tomorrow night and we'll have a good pinochle game or something."

"That sounds like fun," Nellie said, the sparkle coming back into her eyes. "We've been wanting to have you come over for ever so long. Come over and–and we'll have a game of cards or play Scrabble or–or something."

Alex was obviously flustered.

"We'll have to see whether we can make it or not," he said. "I might have to work tomorrow night."

Nellie directed her attention to Robin.

"I've been so anxious to talk to you ever since you kids got married," she said. "Isn't it wonderful to be married?"

Robin nodded.

"I keep telling Joe that being married to him is just like being on one long honeymoon. And I know it must be the same for you kids. Why, we never have a cross word!"

Alex shifted from one foot to the other.

"I think we'd better be going, Robin." He moved off the step. "We don't want to delay Joe and Nellie."

"Oh, you aren't delaying us," Joe said. "We won't be leaving for quite a while yet."

"We'll come back and see you some other time."

"Do that."

It was not until they were back on the sidewalk once more that Robin spoke.

"Oh, Alex," she exclaimed. "I was so ashamed for them."

"Yeah. So was I. And they tried to make us think that everything's so great for them. Boy, if that keeps up, they're going to wind up divorced. That's for sure."

Robin tightened her grip on his arm.

"I'm so glad that no one heard you and me arguing the last few days." There was a short silence. "We're never going to have any trouble again."

CHAPTER 7

GRADUATION BLUES

Graduation night at Fairview High School finally came. Robin had been waiting for it with mixed dread and anticipation. She had wanted to talk with Alex about it, to ask him if he would go with her, but she did not. Instead she waited hopefully.

She half expected that he would plan to work that night, but he came home at the usual time and dropped into a chair in the living room. His hair needed cutting and his hands still bore traces of the grease he had been working in that afternoon.

"Hello, Alex." Robin spoke brightly.

He only grunted in return.

"How did things go at work today?"

"How would you expect things to go at a lousy filling station?" he demanded. "Every character who came in had to have his car greased, the oil changed, or a tire fixed. I'm really beat."

She did not reply.

"Supper ready?" His voice was surly and disgruntled.

"We're eating with Mother and Daddy tonight," she said. "Don't you remember?"

He straightened suddenly.

"How would you expect me to remember? You didn't say anything to me about it."

She came over to his chair.

"I'm sorry, Alex. I really thought I told you."

"Well, you didn't."

"Mother and Daddy asked us to come over this evening and have dinner with them."

He looked at her suspiciously.

"How come?"

"So we can all go to school together."

"And just what gave you the idea that I'm going to graduation tonight?" he demanded heatedly.

Hurt stood in her eyes.

"But you are going, aren't you?"

"Not so anybody could notice!" His voice grated angrily.

"But Alex!" she said plaintively, "I'm graduating tonight, I want you to be there."

He leaped to his feet, eyes blazing.

"I said I'm not going and that's all there is to it. I'm not going." Bitterness galled his words. "You're not going to get me to go to the gym tonight and have everybody there looking at me and wondering why I'm not up there with the rest of the kids. I'm not going. That's final."

She hesitated uneasily.

"If you're not going, I won't go, either."

His temper flared.

"If you think that's going to get me to go, you might just as well save your breath. I told you I'm not going and I'm not. If you don't want to go, stay home. See if I care!"

With that he pivoted on his heel and stormed out of the apartment. Robin's stare followed him. At first, she couldn't believe that he had left without a word. Then tears began to creep, unheeded, down her cheeks.

She stumbled into the bedroom and threw herself across the bed, sobbing. How long she lay there she did not know. It may have been ten minutes. It may have been half an hour. She lay so still one would have thought she was asleep, but she was not.

She half expected Alex to come tiptoeing into the room, remorsefully. She thought he would kiss away her tears and tell her he would go to graduation with her.

But the little upstairs apartment was entirely silent, except for her own muffled sobs and labored breathing. At last, even those sounds ceased, and all was quiet.

Then, she raised up on one elbow and squinted at the clock. It was almost seven! She had no idea it was so late. Her parents were waiting dinner! What could she tell them?

Frantically, she scrambled to her feet and made her way into the bathroom. She scrubbed her face and eyes with cold water in a futile effort to wash away the last traces of her tears. If they asked her why she was late, or where Alex was, she'd tell them. She'd let them see what a spoiled baby he actually was.

It was childish for him to act that way just because he wasn't going to get to graduate. It wasn't her fault she and Alex had gotten married. He had kept coaxing her until finally she gave in. And it wasn't her fault that he had quit school without graduating. She had tried hard enough to keep him from leaving school to take the job at the filling station.

But the way he acted, a person would think she had done everything just to spite him. That she wanted him to be a dropout. And, as if he hadn't done enough, he was trying to get even with her by not going over to see her parents, or to her graduation.

Once more tears welled in her eyes and trickled down her cheeks. Tears of self-pity.

If he wanted to ruin her graduation night, he should be very happy. That's what he had done. He had ruined everything for her.

If it weren't for her parents and the fact that it would hurt them very much if she wasn't there, she wouldn't go herself. She'd stay at home. Maybe that would make him see what he was doing to her.

The corners of her mouth twitched.

When she and Alex had been going together, he was the kindest, most considerate boy she'd ever known. He'd have done anything he could to have kept from hurting her.

But he had certainly changed since they got

married. He was just plain selfish. He knew this should be one of the biggest, most wonderful nights in her whole life. But because he wasn't graduating himself, he couldn't stand to see her happy. He had to do everything he could to ruin it for her.

Only the clock kept her from bursting into tears once more.

Numbly, Robin went over to the closet and examined the dresses that were hanging there. She didn't have a thing she hadn't worn so many times she was ashamed of it.

All the rest of the girls would have new dresses tonight. She had seen Linda Penner going home from town that afternoon with a dress box under her arm. She had been so ashamed that she wasn't going to have a new dress, she had turned and walked a block out of her way to keep from meeting Linda on the street.

And it wasn't only Linda who would have a new dress. So would every other girl in the whole graduating class. Every other girl except her.

Robin's lips began to quiver once more.

It had been so long since she had a new dress that she had forgotten what it was like. She hadn't bought one single new thing since she and Alex were married. They never had money enough to buy anything except what they really needed.

A numb ache took hold of her as she selected one of the dresses from her closet, got into it, and began to pull a comb through her hair.

What difference did it make whether she looked nice or not? Alex wouldn't be there to see her.

CHAPTER 8

A CONFESSION

Danny and Kay Orlis went to the graduation exercises at the high school gymnasium that night, as did almost everyone else in Fairview. When the address by the visiting dignitary dragged to a close and the last senior received his diploma, they got to their feet.

"Didn't Robin look sweet?" Kay asked.

"I thought she looked sad and upset about something."

"I imagine it was Alex. Did you see him here tonight?"

He shook his head.

At that moment Mr. and Mrs. Evans came over and spoke to them.

"We'd like to have you come over for a cup of coffee, Danny," Richard Evans said.

"Yes," his wife put in. "It's been such a long time since we've been able to visit with you."

Danny glanced at his wife.

"What do you think about going out this evening, Kay?"

"If you don't think it would be too late, Danny, I think I'd like to. Like Gladys says, it has been a long time."

"I won't be flying tomorrow, as far as I know." He directed his attention to Richard Evans. "Thanks for asking us, Dick. We'll stop by for a little while."

"Good. If you get there before we do, go right in and make yourselves at home. We'll be there in just a little while.

In the Evans' living room, the conversation turned, inevitably, to the graduation exercises that evening.

"It was so nice," Kay said. "And Robin looked so pretty."

"It was very nice," Gladys Evans answered, her fingers working nervously. "But I can tell you this much. It has been something of an ordeal for us. Both Richard and I have been dreading tonight."

"I don't believe 1 follow you," Danny answered.

"We had such high hopes for Robin and what she would be making of her life," Richard Evans went on, pouring a spoonful of cream in his coffee. "But it turned out very different for us than we thought it would."

Gladys' lower lip quivered, as though she was about to cry.

"Parents usually look forward to the graduation of their children," she said. "It's somewhat of a milestone. You feel as though you've really accomplished something." Her voice choked and it was a long while before she could go on. "We had thought it would be the beginning of three or four happy, carefree years at Bible school for Robin."

"That's right." Remorse crept into Richard's voice. "Now, of course, that's completely out of the question."

"And to make it even worse, Alex had to quit school and wasn't able to graduate tonight."

"We weren't going to say anything, but I guess there's no point in trying to keep it a secret. Alex stormed out of their apartment this evening without any supper and didn't come back. He said he wasn't going to come to the graduation services, and he didn't."

Kay smiled understandingly.

"I would imagine it's been a very difficult evening for him. I'm sure he has felt much worse about quitting school than he would ever let anyone know."

Mrs. Evans nodded.

"I'm quite certain of that." There was a long, painful silence. "If anybody would have told Richard and me a year ago that Robin would be married by the time she graduated, we would have told them that they didn't know our little girl." She shook her head in disbelief. "And the worst of it is that the boy she's married to isn't even a Christian and won't go to Sunday school or church or anything."

Richard sighed deeply.

"Danny," he began. "I'm frank to admit that I don't understand what's taken place. I don't know what happened to our girl. At one time she was a sweet, considerate, consecrated Christian. I thought we were one pair of parents who weren't going to have any trouble with their daughter."

"We just didn't know," his wife put in.

"Actually, we didn't have any trouble with her until shortly after the school year started last fall. Then she started going with Alex. It wasn't long until she was deceiving us in every way possible. And–." He swallowed hard. "And now, this. It almost seems as though God is punishing us for something."

His wife eyed him quickly.

"Just what do you mean by that, Richard?"

He was a long while in answering.

"I've been doing a lot of thinking about Robin and Alex the past few weeks. I've been trying to figure out why things turned out the way they did."

"It was certainly none of our doing," his wife retorted. "We tried every way possible to show her how she should live as a Christian. We even got her that car."

Richard scarcely heard her.

"I've asked myself a thousand times why she became so rebellious and defiant," he went on. "What was it that made her change?" He expelled his breath slowly.

"It must be the influence of the school and the other kids. If she could just have associated with Christians all the time, we wouldn't have the situation we've got now."

"I'm not sure that's it, Gladys." Richard turned to Danny. "I always come back to the same thing. Robin wanted to go to the mission field and we weren't willing to let her. We wanted her to live for the Lord, but we were determined in our own mind and heart that we were going to dictate how and where she was to be used. We weren't going to let the Lord use her any place other than Fairfield."

His wife spoke up sharply.

"But, Richard," she exclaimed, "Robin couldn't possibly have gone to the mission field. She–she's always been too delicate and frail for that." Tears came to her voice. "Her health would break under it and–."

Richard Evans' face was serious.

"We might just as well face up to it, Dear," he said hoarsely. "That's not the reason we didn't want her to go to the mission field. Not the real reason."

"And just what do you mean by that?"

"You know as well as I do, what I mean. Even though Robin has been thin, she's always been as healthy as a colt. It wasn't her health that made us so set against her becoming a missionary. We were selfish. We didn't want her to leave Fairview. That's the brutal truth of the matter."

His wife's temper blazed.

"Robin's the only child we have. Is it so wrong to want to live close to her?"

Richard leaned forward slightly. His entire body was tense, and his gaze burned into that of his wife.

"Answer me one question, Gladys," he said in soft tones. "Do we have Robin now?"

She began to sniffle.

"I–I don't think I know what you mean."

"I think you do." He waited while his words soaked in. "There's a wall between Robin and Alex, and you and me. A wall that separates us from Robin more surely than if she were ten thousand miles away."

"I don't feel that way at all," she whimpered, but her very tone gave away the lie in her words.

"I'd give anything in the world if we could go back to the way Robin was a year ago," Richard said, sighing wearily. "If only we had another chance to give her our permission to follow the Lord's leading. If we could have another chance to help her go to the mission field where God was calling her."

Mrs. Evans wiped at the tears in her eyes with trembling fingers.

"But–."

"We couldn't entrust her to the care of God. We had to have our own way with Robin." His lips curled bitterly.

"I suppose you're blaming me for it," Gladys said.

"I'm blaming myself. And now there isn't a thing we can do about it. Robin isn't serving the Lord, but we don't have her, either." He took a long breath. "And what's almost as bad, she seems to be miserable in the bargain. The way things are, nobody has gained."

Danny fumbled hesitantly for words.

How could he answer Richard, except to agree with him? Gladys made a feeble attempt to change the subject, but it was useless. Nobody felt like visiting after what had taken place. In half an hour or so Danny and Kay excused themselves and went home.

Mr. and Mrs. Evans remained on the porch after their guests were gone. At last Gladys turned to her husband.

"Richard," she said, her voice weak.

"Yes?"

"Richard, I–" She fought against the lump in her throat.

"What is it, Dear?"

"I've been thinking about what you said a little while ago."

"I'm sorry if I hurt you. I didn't mean to. I was really just talking to myself. Trying to get things worked out in my own mind."

"You don't have to apologize. I don't like to admit it, but what you said a little while ago is true. We–." Tears began to flow, shamelessly.

"Don't do that, Gladys. You're just torturing yourself."

"Don't stop me," she continued. "I've got to say it." There was a brief pause.

"We were so selfish in insisting that Robin stay at home. God knew what was best for her, and for us, too. Yet we couldn't let Him have His way, so He let us have our way. And this is what happened."

Richard put his arm around his wife's shoulder and drew her close.

"I know it," he admitted. "I know it as surely as I've ever known anything in my life."

"Do you suppose God can forgive us?" she asked, tremulously.

He squeezed her shoulder reassuringly.

"Of course, He can forgive us, Dear. He always forgives those who come to Him and ask for forgiveness.

Her lower lip quivered.

"I know He will," she repeated. "I shouldn't even have asked that. But our being forgiven isn't going to straighten out Robin's life. I–I'm afraid she'll never have the opportunity to get into the center of His will again."

They went into the house together and dropped to their knees. For a long while they knelt, pouring out their hearts to God. When at last they got to their feet, Mrs. Evans was smiling slightly.

"I do feel better now," she acknowledged.

"So do I," her husband said. "Or at least I will feel better when we've talked to Robin about this and have asked her forgiveness. We've sinned grievously against her."

CHAPTER 9

NO MORE EXCUSES

Kay had spent the day before getting Jim Morgan's things ready for him to go to Canada with the Cedarton Bible Institute work crew. She washed and ironed all his clothes and supervised his packing. She planned on going back home and lying down for a while, but on impulse she stopped at Alex and Robin's apartment. Even though it was almost noon, Robin was just finishing the breakfast dishes when Kay knocked at the door.

"Hello, Robin."

"Hello."

She tried to match her caller's gaiety, but somehow it did not come off. Her face was drawn and white and dark circles ringed her eyes.

"I just dropped Jim off at the bus depot."

Kay dropped wearily into a chair.

"And I don't mind telling you that I'm about beat."

A long sigh escaped her lips. "Robin, you can't imagine how helpless a boy like that can be."

"Oh, can't I?" she demanded, her voice rising. "You happen to forget that I'm married to one."

Kay laughed.

In the short silence that followed Robin looked apologetically at the dishes in the sink. "I–I should have had the dishes done by this time. Alex will be home in a little while for lunch." Hurt twisted her face. "That is, if he comes home at all."

Surprised, Kay looked up quickly.

"Does Alex take his lunch to the station with him?" she asked.

Robin's mouth twitched convulsively, and she was fighting to keep back the tears.

"I–I guess there's no use trying to hide it. Alex and I had another terrible argument this morning." She dabbed at her eyes with a tissue. "This was the worst one yet."

"Oh, that's too bad."

"I can't figure out what's the matter with him, Kay," she said. "Ever since graduation he's been furious at me. And just over nothing! I think he's actually jealous of the fact that I stayed in school and got my diploma. I think he's mad because I didn't quit the same time he did."

"I don't think he's jealous of you, Robin," she replied. "Not really. And I'm sure he does feel terrible about not getting his diploma with the rest of the class."

Robin left the sink and came over to where Kay was sitting.

"But it wasn't my fault that he quit school and didn't graduate. I didn't have anything to do with it. But he acts as though I did. To hear him you'd think I tricked him into quitting school just to spite him."

She swallowed the lump in her throat.

"Now he's talking as though he might get a job with a construction gang and leave Fairview for the summer and–"

She started to cry once more.

Kay went over to her and put her arm around the girl's frail shoulders.

"I'm sure he didn't mean that," she said.

But Robin was unconvinced.

"You don't know how he is when he gets mad. You don't know what he'll do."

Kay guided her to the sofa and sat down beside her. It was several minutes before she quit crying and was able to talk again.

"I–I love Alex, Kay," she began, her voice quavering thinly. "I love him more than anyone else in the whole world, but–." She swallowed hard.

"But what?"

"I–I just didn't think there could be so many problems involved in marriage. Nobody ever told us that it was going to be like this."

Kay nodded.

"Marriage is a serious matter," she said. "A very serious matter. And any couple has to work hard at it to make it successful."

"If only Alex had graduated from high school and had gone on to college or had some sort of training to help him get a better job. That would make everything so much easier for us both than it is now."

Kay nodded.

"I'm sure it would."

"And if I knew more about cleaning house and cooking and–." She grasped Kay's arm. "I never dreamed that there could be so much work involved in keeping a little apartment the way it should be kept."

Kay smiled.

"I think that's something that surprises every girl when she gets married. I thought I never would be able to organize my work so I could keep it up. In fact, it gets me bogged down every once in a while, even now."

Clouds came back to the younger girl's eyes.

"But it was different for you when you got married. All the girls my age are going to parties now, or are going out on dates and having fun. If they want to sleep until noon, they can. And if they have a job they usually can spend as much of their wages as they want to on clothes and pretty, silly little things."

She paused.

"Everyone my age can do that, except me. I never get to go anywhere."

Kay was not sympathetic. "That's part of the price of getting married. A married girl just doesn't have the freedom to do the things a single girl has. There's no escaping it."

Tears trickled down Robin's cheeks once more.

"We–we probably wouldn't have gotten married at all if it hadn't been for Mother and Daddy," she complained. "They were so unreasonable about letting me date Alex that we practically had to run away and get married."

Kay scowled her disapproval.

"I don't think you're being fair to your parents, Robin."

The hurt flamed in the younger girl's eyes.

"I think I am. Do you realize that Alex was the first boy I'd ever gone with who wasn't a Christian?"

Kay nodded.

"And I didn't start going with him until after they got me the car so H wouldn't go to the mission field," she continued. "They even admitted that it was all their fault. They both came over to see me yesterday and asked for my forgiveness."

She paused significantly, as though that proved her own lack of responsibility in the matter.

"Danny and I talked to your parents on graduation night. They both indicated that they feel responsible for what happened. They feel that if they had allowed you to follow the Lord's will, you would be in Bible school today and not married to Alex."

"That's what I've been trying to tell you."

"But that doesn't wipe out your personal responsibility before God in the matter."

Robin's lips trembled and she moistened them uneasily with the tip of her tongue.

"Wh–what do you mean?"

"The Bible tells us that we're responsible for our own actions. God wasn't calling your parents to the mission field, Robin," she said. "He was calling you. Your parents didn't like it that you were going to be a missionary and tried to get you to change your mind, but you are the one who made the decision to turn your back on God's call."

"But–."

"Your mother and dad would not have interfered if you had gone to them in sincerity and love, and explained your call to them and told them you had to follow God. They probably would have felt badly for a time, but they wouldn't have hindered you."

Robin said nothing.

"And," Kay went on, "you are the one who is going to have to pay the price for choosing God's second or third or fourth best for your life."

"But if they hadn't interfered, I'd have gone to Bible school to prepare myself for missionary work," the girl protested.

In spite of Robin's indignation and attempts to persuade her, Kay did not relent.

"The Bible is very clear in telling us what to do when we're faced with a situation like this," she said. "When you had opposition at home you should have asked the Lord for strength to help you do what He wanted you to do, instead of giving in to pressure."

"But–." Robin began to cry once more. This time

there was penitence in her voice when she spoke. "I–I've tried and tried to make excuses for myself, but down deep in my heart I know that what you're saying is true. Will God forgive me, Kay?"

Kay enveloped the crying girl in her arms.

"Of course, He will."

Together they knelt in prayer.

CHAPTER 10

THE COACH'S ASSISTANT

Life did not change very much for Alex and Robin during the summer months, except that it was much easier for Robin to keep up with her housework now that she didn't have to go to school. She was learning a little more about cleaning and cooking, and had even gotten herself a part-time job as a clerk in the local discount store. Her pay was low, but it did help to relieve their tight financial situation a bit.

Alex seemed happier than usual now that there was a little more money coming in. At least, he was happier until the football season came along. Then he became morose and grouchy. Robin noticed it almost immediately and was concerned about it.

"Alex," she said tenderly, "what's the matter?" She went over and sat on the arm of his chair.

Ignoring her, he opened the paper to the sports page and pretended to read.

"What's wrong?" she repeated.

"Nothing." He clipped off the word decisively. "Nothing at all."

"I know better. There's something troubling you."

"There isn't anything the matter. It's just your imagination."

She tangled her fingers in his hair. He pulled slightly away from her.

"Kay stopped in at the store this afternoon," Robin said presently.

He scowled. "What'd she want? Is she still tryin' to get me to go to that stupid church of yours?"

His young wife bristled. "That wasn't why she came by at all. She didn't say a word about church. As a matter of fact, she knew you liked football. So she stopped in to see if we wanted their tickets for the game tonight. They aren't going to be able to go."

He brightened noticeably. "Hey, that sounds all right. It's been a long time since I saw a football game." He got to his feet. "We're going to have to hurry. There'll be a big crowd out there tonight and we want to get there early enough to get a good seat."

They were both getting ready to go to the game when he spoke again. "Know something, Robin?" he said. "At this time last year, I thought I was going to be playing on the freshman football team at the university this season."

She winced at the note of longing in his voice.

"Don't feel so bad about it," she said.

He sighed again. "I don't feel so bad, I guess. At

least if I had to take my choice, I'd rather be married to you, even though it meant that I'd never see another football. But we might just as well face it, a guy can't help feeling a little upset over not getting to play a game he likes as well as I like football."

Impulsively she turned, flashing him a quick smile. "I understand, Alex. And I'm glad that you'd rather be married to me than be playing football." Her face grew serious. "I only wish that you hadn't had to make the choice the way you did."

"Now don't go worrying about that," he said as though it didn't matter to him. "I'll live without football. That's for sure."

They walked across town to the football field, arriving a few minutes before kickoff.

Fairview started the first quarter shakily. Although they won the toss and elected to receive, they lost the ball on the second play and Roscoe scored early in the first quarter. Jim Morgan, who had done a very acceptable job the first two games of the season, was having trouble.

Alex groaned.

"Just look at the way Jim's playing," he muttered under his breath. "He's sure fouling up tonight."

A voice behind him spoke. He turned to see one of his former high school instructors. "We might just as well face it, Alex," he said. "They don't play the game the way you did last year."

The boy's face muscles tightened. "I wish I was out there, believe me!"

"You and me both. That Roscoe outfit hasn't got such a good team. We're just making a lot of mistakes. That's all."

Fairview tried to run off another play, but it was fumbled just as he was getting under way, and just managed to recover it himself.

Alex turned to Robin. "Watch Jim Morgan," he said. "He's tipping off every move he makes. On this play he's going to pull out and come around to run interference around the weak side of the line."

Sure enough. The ball was snapped to Fritz McCloud who took two or three quick steps backward and flipped the ball to the quarterback who started around the weak side of the line. Jim pulled out to run interference but scarcely reached his position when the Roscoe line swarmed in and smothered both him and the ballcarrier.

Alex groaned again. "See, what did I tell you?"

It was much the same on defense. Jim wasn't able to get in on more than a small handful of plays. And when the game was over, Fairview had been defeated by six points. On the way home all Alex could talk about were the stupid mistakes Jim Morgan had made.

"I don't care what he thinks about it, Robin," Alex said at last. "I'm going to go over and tell him what he's doing wrong. There's no excuse for a guy who should be good playing football that way."

"Don't you think it's the coach's place to tell him?"

Alex snorted.

* * *

Robin hoped that Alex would forget about talking to Jim Morgan about his mistakes on the football field, but such was not the case. The next afternoon he saw the high schooler on the street and called to him. Jim came over to where Alex was standing.

"Hi, Alex," he said warmly. "How're you these days?"

The older boy ignored his question. "I saw you play football last night," he said.

Jim's smile faded. "It was a lousy game, wasn't it?"

"You can say that again. It was no wonder you didn't win. Of all the lousy playing I've ever seen, you guys beat the lot. You were terrible."

His voice was harsh and accusing, more bitter than he wanted it to be. Briefly, Jim's temper flared in return, but when he spoke, he was able to control himself.

"You're not telling me anything. It seemed to me that I couldn't do anything right last night. I was clobbered every time I turned around.

Alex expelled his breath slowly. "Didn't anybody tell you what you were doing wrong?"

Jim laughed. "Coach Harper did have a few hundred choice words about how lousy I was doing."

"It's no wonder you guys couldn't get your plays to click. You were tipping off every single play you made."

Jim's forehead creased. "What do you mean by that?"

"You mean you don't know?" Sarcasm was thick in Alex' voice.

"Listen, Alex. I really don't know very much about this game. I didn't even make the starting lineup until Paul got hurt. Then the coach had to put me in. If there's something you can tell me that'll help me play my position any better, I'd certainly appreciate it."

Alex drew in his breath sharply. This was something he had not been expecting. He had thought Jim would get mad and snap back at him. The anger and accusation left his voice.

"Oh, I suppose it would be easy for you to miss what I'm talking about. And I imagine it would be easy for the coach to miss it on the bench. But we were sitting quite high in the stands and I was able to spot it right off."

"Spot what?"

"You were telegraphing every play an instant before the ball was snapped. Why, I told both Robin and Mr. Tucker exactly what you were going to do before the plays even started."

Surprise flickered in Jim's eyes. "You don't mean it."

"I sure do mean it. You were telegraphing the plays with your actions. The Roscoe line could watch you and get a good idea of where the ball was going by the way you looked or shifted your feet." Quickly he related several incidents to show what he meant.

Jim pulled in a deep breath. "I wasn't even aware that I was moving at all before the ball was snapped."

"I didn't think you were," Alex went on. "It's easy to get into habits like that. It happened to me when I was a sophomore trying to make the team. I was so tense and eager that I developed all sorts of little habits before the ball was snapped."

"How's a guy going to break himself of that sort of thing?" Jim wanted to know.

Alex paused momentarily. "If you'd like to work on those things, I'll try to help you as much as I can. I know what our coach used to do to help me."

The Morgan boy's eyes lit. "Would you?" he echoed. "That'd be great!"

"Sure, I'll help you. I get off work just about the time you finish football practice. If you'd like to stop by the apartment for a while after supper, I think I can help you."

"I'll be there Monday night. You can count on that." His grin widened. "Thanks a lot!"

When Alex got home from work that evening, he expressed his surprise at Jim's attitude to Robin.

"You know," he told her, "it just about floored me when he didn't get mad. I thought he'd tell me to mind my own business and stay out of his affairs, but he didn't. He acted as though he was real glad that I'd told him what he was doing to give away the plays."

Robin smiled. "I'm not at all surprised that Jim didn't get mad when you talked with him, Alex. He's a Christian."

Her young husband's mouth tightened, and his eyes flashed their warning. "Being a Christian doesn't have a thing to do with it. He just wants to learn to play football better than he does, and he knows that I can help him, that's all."

On Monday and Tuesday nights Jim went over to Alex and Robin's apartment and he and Alex went over his problems in detail. "I watched you during the game, Jim," Alex said, "and it seemed to me that you always did the same thing just before any certain play. For example, your body tenses when you're going to run interference for the ballcarrier. You don't do that when you're going to decoy."

"I sure didn't know I was doing anything different," he said.

"And," Alex continued, "you've got a habit of shifting your foot in the direction you're going to be running just before the ball is snapped. An alert lineman could watch you and figure out just what you're going to do." The older boy paused. "And of course, a tip-off like that can help a lot in figuring out what the play is going to be and where it's going."

The Morgan boy nodded. "I'm sure glad you told me about it. If you hadn't, I might have gone through the whole season without knowing why our plays were getting messed up so often."

Alex nodded. "That's right.' A grin lit his face. "You know, I just thought of something, Jim. If anybody was scouting Fairview Friday night, they probably caught what you were doing. If they did, they'll be looking for you to tip off the plays. You can cross them up for a little while, anyway, by looking in the opposite direction you plan to go, and by mixing up these things you've been doing."

Carefully Alex drilled Jim until both of them were sure that the habit was completely broken.

"I sure wish you could come out and watch our scrimmage tomorrow night," Jim said gratefully. "I'd like to have you see whether I'm making any improvement."

"You'll make improvement, all right, if you remember what I've been telling you."

The following afternoon Jim's play was so much sharper than it had been before that everyone noticed it. Coach Harper stopped the scrimmage and came over to him.

"You're doing great, Jim," he said. "You're really coming alive this evening."

The Morgan boy grinned. "Alex Smith has been helping me with a few problems I've had." Briefly he told the coach what had taken place.

"Sometimes that sort of thing is difficult to spot from the bench," the coach replied, pulling thoughtfully at the lobe of his ear. "But he must be sharp on his football to have spotted that from the stands. Did I understand you to say that he noticed it the first game he watched you play?"

"That's right."

There was a brief silence. "I think I'm going down and have a little talk with him. We could use a guy like him to help us with the coaching for the rest of the season. He could probably show all the guys a few things about playing their positions."

The following morning on the way to school Stan Harper stopped by the filling station and talked with Alex. "I want to tell you how much I appreciate your help with Jim Morgan. I think he's going to be able to play his position a lot better because of your work with him."

Alex grinned broadly. "Well, I just couldn't stand to see him lousing things up the way he was. He might as well have been wearing a signboard telling what the play was going to be."

"How about you coming out and giving the other boys a few pointers?" the coach asked. "I think some of the things they need to be told would mean a lot more to them coming from someone like you instead of me."

Alex' face grew somber. "I'd sure like to do that, Mr. Harper," he said wistfully. "I'd like that more than anything I know of, but I'm afraid that my boss wouldn't let me."

"Maybe he wouldn't," the coach said, "and maybe he would. Why don't you let me go over and have a talk with him?"

Alex thought for a moment. "I suppose it would be all right if you're sure to tell him it's all your idea. If I lost my job, I'd really be in the soup."

"I won't cause you any trouble in that department. You can be sure of that."

That afternoon Alex' boss called him into the office and told him that he was going to let him off for a couple of hours every afternoon until the end of the football season. "Coach Harper seems to think that you can do a lot for our football team, Alex."

"I'll sure do my best to help them."

"Oh, yes. You won't be losing any salary. I decided to make your wages for the time you're helping the guys my contribution to the team."

The boy grinned his appreciation.

CHAPTER 11

BACK TO SCHOOL

Alex left the station Thursday afternoon shortly before four o'clock and went out to the football field for the light drill they always had the day before a game. He talked with the guys about the importance of giving their best and working for the team.

"It doesn't make any difference how good you are," he began. "If you can't play with the other ten guys on the team, you aren't going to be worth much to Fairview High. You've got to forget about who carries the ball and gets the headlines. The guys who block are as important as the ballcarriers. It's the team that counts."

When he finished, Coach Harper nodded approvingly. "I don't think I can add a thing to what has been said," he concluded. "I'm going to be watching tomorrow night to see if you really put Alex' little talk into practice."

Fairview seemed to be revitalized as they went out on the football field Friday night and beat Glenville handily. Jim Morgan made more blocks than he had in any other game they'd played and was important in helping to smother the opposition's passing attack. There was no question about it. It was the best game that he had ever played.

When the final gun sounded, Coach Harper gave Alex credit for the change. "I want to thank you again for the way you helped Jim. I didn't think he would ever be able to play as well as he played tonight."

"I'm sure glad I was able to help him a little. Jim's a nice guy."

Alex could scarcely wait for Monday afternoon to come so he could go out to the football practice field again. Coach Harper was waiting for him. "I've got some work I want to do with the line today," he said. "Would you take the backfield and try to sharpen up the way they execute the plays?"

"Sure thing." He raised his voice. "Come on, you guys. We've got some work to do!"

For the next couple of hours, he drilled them as hard as they had ever been drilled in their lives. Every now and then Coach Harper came over, listened for a time, made a suggestion or two, and went back to working with the line. For the most part he left Alex alone. When the practice session was over a few minutes after six o'clock, he walked back to the locker room with his youthful helper.

"How're you coming on the plays?"

"OK," the boy answered. "I worked most of yesterday on them. I think I'll have them memorized in a couple of days."

"Good. I think you'll be even more help to us when you get all the plays memorized." At the door he paused. "The guys are looking better. You're going to be a big help to us, Alex."

"Thank you." His smile was broad.

Around home Alex was different than he had been for months. He joked a lot and insisted on telling Robin everything that had taken place. She had all but lost interest in football, but now that Alex was helping with the team, she was more interested than she had ever been.

"How's Jim coming along?" she asked.

"He's going to be all right," Alex said. "He's a great competitor and will listen when I tell him what to do. I think we can make a good football player out of him."

Robin smiled gratefully. It was so good to see Alex like this. He was more like the Alex she had known when they were going together the year before.

* * *

Although Stanley Harper was a football coach of exceptional ability, Alex seemed to make the difference between victory and defeat in the last three games Fairview played. They were bitterly fought contests that could have gone either way until the closing moments of the last quarter. But Fairview came clawing back to eke out the few points necessary for winning.

The football coach was deeply appreciative for the help Alex gave the team. And in the locker room after the next to the last game of the season he held out his hand.

"I guess you know how grateful I am for the way you've helped us, Alex," he said.

"I was glad to do it." Slowly his smile faded. "As a matter of fact, I'm sorry it's almost over."

"If you're going to be around next year, I'd like to speak now for your services. I think we could do an even better job after having worked together this year."

Hurt flashed deep in the boy's eyes. "I'll probably be here, all right," he replied. "There's not much chance I'd have of being anywhere else."

"I thought you'd probably go on to school somewhere."

Alex laughed dryly. "Fat chance of that."

"You should go on to school, you know," Mr. Harper told him seriously. "You have the natural qualifications to make a good coach."

Alex did not reply.

"One of these times I'd like to have you come into my office and talk to me, Alex," Harper went on. "I'm serious about this. Why don't you go to college and get your degree so you can become a coach?"

The boy flinched as though he had been hit in the face. "That's just about impossible."

"With a guy your age who really wants to do it, it's not impossible at all. There's not a thing wrong with working in a filling station. It's a good, honorable job. But Alex, you've got a natural ability to coach. I'd hate to see you give up so easily."

There was a brief silence.

"I'll tell you what, Mr. Harper," Alex said. "I'll come into your office some time and tell you why it's impossible for me to think about coaching."

With that he turned on his heel and stormed out into the chilling night. Robin, who had been waiting for him near the gate, looked up as he approached.

"Oh, Alex," she began as he came up to her, "I was so proud of the boys and the way they played tonight."

He said nothing.

"Everybody in the stands was talking about the improvement they've made in the past few days. I felt like standing up and shouting that it was because you're helping coach the team."

Alex grunted under his breath. "Coach Harper's plenty good. The guys just found themselves, that's all."

"Mrs. Harper told me that the coach felt you have had as much to do with this season's victories as anyone else."

Alex did not answer her. Instead, he picked up a twig, broke it in two as they walked, and threw it savagely to the ground. When they got home, he stalked into the apartment, dropped heavily to a chair near the radio, and stared bleakly off into space.

Robin came into the room some minutes later and saw that he had not moved. "Alex," she said, "is there something wrong?"

He glowered at her without speaking.

"Did something go wrong on the job today?" she persisted.

His scowl deepened, and when he spoke, he spat out the words. "What could go wrong with a stinkin' filling station job?"

Her own anger flared in response to his. "I'm sorry I asked."

Alex picked up the paper, unfolded it, and tried to read the headlines on the sports page. But the letters all ran together in a meaningless jumble. Finally he put the paper aside.

He had enjoyed helping coach the football team more than anything else he'd ever done. And Coach Harper said he had natural ability as a coach.

A great longing swept over him. A longing to go on to school, to get his degree and a job coaching. But how could he manage that? He didn't even have his high school diploma, let alone a college degree. And, as if that wasn't enough, he had a wife to support.

He was trapped! Trapped!

* * *

A day or so before the final football game of the season Coach Harper phoned Alex at work and asked him to stop by the school.

"I'd like to talk to you, Alex."

"Maybe I can take a few minutes off my lunch hour and see you."

"I'll be waiting for you."

An hour or so later Alex was at the coach's office.

"I've been doing a lot of thinking about you the last few days, Alex," he began. "I think you owe it to yourself and the coaching profession to go to college, get your degree, and become a coach."

The corners of the boy's mouth drew down to a thin, hard line. "I wish I could," he said fervently. "Believe me, I wish I could. That's all I've thought about since you talked to me a few days ago. But it's no use. I can't go on to school. I don't have a high school diploma and I've got a wife to support."

"I know all that," Mr. Harper answered. "But I still think it's possible. You only lack a semester of high school, right? If you really want to, you can make that up."

"How? By going back to school with the kids who're there now? No, thanks."

"Have you ever thought of the adult education program?"

Alex' forehead crinkled. "Adult education? All they teach is typing and Spanish or French, don't they?"

The coach shook his head. "Oh, no. They have an entire high school program now. And the nice thing about it is that a person can go as fast as he wants to. If you really set your mind to it, you could probably make up that semester in three months or so."

Alex' eyes lighted. "Do you really think so?"

Coach Harper nodded for emphasis. "I not only think it, I know it. You wouldn't have any trouble at all. You'd only have to give up about three nights a week and do some studying two or three other nights. You wouldn't find it any trouble."

Alex could scarcely believe it was true. Slowly he turned the matter over in his mind. "Even if I did get my diploma," he said, "I'd still have four years of college to go. I could never make that and still take care of Robin."

"I don't know why you can't. I was married the last two years I went to college. It was tough. I won't try to kid you about that. But it can be done, Alex. There's only one thing that would stop you."

"What's that?"

"You and your wife have to want it badly enough to make the sacrifices. If you do, you've got it made."

When Alex got home that evening, he talked with Robin about it. "Coach Harper seems to think I could go on to college and become a coach," he said hesitantly, watching her reaction.

Her eyes brightened. "Oh, Alex!" she exclaimed. "That would be wonderful!"

"It would be tough on both of us. You'd probably have to work and so would I. And we wouldn't have any money to spend foolishly."

"Oh, that wouldn't make any difference to me. I've got some experience clerking in a store now. When you go on to college, I could get a job of some kind to help out."

Alex' smile was filled with hope and anticipation.

"I'd about given up the idea of ever getting a college education."

"So had I." Her voice raised in new gaiety. "Why, Alex, it will be an answer to prayer!"

He did not reply.

The following day after school Coach Harper stopped at the station and had Alex fill his car with gas. When the boy had finished, he handed him a leaflet.

"I talked with one of the teachers in the Adult Education Program," he began. "He gave me the material on their courses. I thought maybe you'd like to take it home and look it over."

"Thanks." His face beamed. "Thanks a lot."

That evening he and Robin studied the material together. Before long they had decided on his going to night classes to get his diploma and then going on to college.

"In looking over these courses, I don't think I'll have any trouble with them. Why, I did a good share of the work before I dropped out my senior year. I should be able to sail through that far."

He took the application and sat down at the kitchen table to fill it out. Robin went into the bedroom and knelt beside the bed. She hadn't been so genuinely happy and relieved since they had been married. And she knew her parents were going to be as thrilled as she was. She didn't know how long she remained on her knees, but Alex had finished filling out the application and was walking around the kitchen when she got to her feet.

That night she lay awake for a long while planning just what she would say to Alex about going to church with her the following Sunday. She figured out exactly how she should approach him and what she would say to convince him he should go with her.

All Alex really needed to be the perfect husband was to accept Christ as his Savior. And now she was positive that was going to happen. God was finally going to answer her prayers and make her husband exactly what he should be.

When she got up the following morning, she was so happy she could scarcely contain herself. She sang as she got breakfast and set the table. Alex came into the kitchen, eyeing her curiously.

"Say, you're bright and cheery this morning. What happened? Did someone leave you a million dollars?"

She flashed a quick grin. "I don't think I'd be as happy if they had."

He studied her youthful face. "Does my going back to school mean so much to you?" he asked.

"It means everything to me." And then, because it was so heavy on her mind, she asked him about going to church with her on Sunday. "In thanksgiving for what happened, Alex," she said, "I thought it would be nice if we could go to church together."

His eyes grew hard, and his voice was like cold, rolled steel. "How many times do I have to tell you, Robin?" he lashed. "I don't want anything to do with your religion, and I'm sick and tired of having you nag me about it."

Her lips trembled. "But Alex, when we were married you promised me that you would go to church with me."

"I have been to church with you. Now stop this nagging and leave me alone!" He went into the bathroom and a moment or two later she heard the water running in the shower.

Miserably she dropped to a chair. What was the matter with Alex, anyway? He was the kindest, most gentle, most considerate husband any girl could ask for most of the time. That is, until she mentioned something about going to church, or reading the Bible, or asking Pastor Reeves or Danny and Kay to come over. Then it seemed that his entire personality changed.

Silently, she started to cry. It was so hard to have a husband who didn't know the Lord Jesus Christ as his Savior. Harder than she had ever dreamed it could be!

* * *

Jim Morgan played his best game of the year against neighboring Canfield. The visitors had trampled all the competition in sight and the newspapers freely predicted a three touchdown rout. But at half-time Fairview led 7-0, and when the final gun sounded, they had eked out a narrow 7-6 victory. Jubilantly Coach Harper led his squad into the dressing room.

"You guys were terrific tonight! Absolutely terrific!"

The guys showered and started to dress. Jim was tying his shoes when he turned to the guy next to him.

"Did you get a date tonight for after the game?" He nodded his head.

"Did you ask Peggy Merrill?"

"I asked her, all right, but she informed me that she's now going steady with Dick Butler and won't be able to go out with me anymore."

"Butler?" Jim echoed. "When'd she start going with him?"

"Search me."

"That's tough."

"Oh, it's not so bad. I got a date with Sally Elwood."

Alex left the locker room about the same time as Jim, and when he got home Robin was already there.

"It was a good game, Alex," she said.

"It sure was." He eyed her quizzically. "What're you doing?"

In spite of herself, her cheeks flushed. "I'm just working on a little correspondence course."

"What kind of a correspondence course?"

"It's one I got from CBI – a missionary course." The frown lines on his young face deepened. "Missionary course?" Derision curled his lips. "How come you're doing a stupid thing like that?"

Robin winced.

CHAPTER 12

PEGGY'S DECISION

Alex and Robin had a measure of happiness, she realized all too well that it was limited. Most of the time she tried to ignore it, but she was uneasily aware of the fact that there was a permanent barrier that kept them from getting close together – a barrier that kept them from experiencing the same sort of happiness that Danny and Kay had.

She loved Alex deeply. That was very true. But all of this must be God's second best for her. Small wonder there was an emptiness within, an unsatisfied hunger to be one with God.

It seemed that she would never get to sleep that night, and when she awoke in the morning, the ache was still in her heart.

Alex, however, seemed happier than he had ever been.

"I sure didn't realize how much my dropping out of school was bothering me, Robin," he said. "Now that I've started work on my night courses I feel as though I just got out of jail or something."

Robin smiled. "I know just how you must feel, and I'm just as happy for you."

"It's going to be tough going to school and supporting a wife at the same time," he said. His expression changed and he reached out, impulsively, to lay his hand on hers. "It's going to be tough for you, too. I know that. But I'll make it all up to you someday."

"If you stick it out until you get your college degree, you'll more than make it up to me, Alex," she said. "That's what I want more than anything else."

There was new determination in his voice. "You won't have to worry about that. I'll stick it out. With a wife like you, how could I miss?"

He leaned over and kissed her lightly on the cheek. "Aren't you glad we got married when we did?"

His words stabbed into her heart. She tried to answer him, but in spite of herself, she could not. Fortunately, Alex was in such a gay, outgoing mood that he didn't notice.

"I've got to get down to the station. Sweetie. See you at noon."

At the door he turned back momentarily. "You think about dropping that silly Bible course and taking a course with me at night school. It'd do us both good."

For half a minute she stared after him. He expected her not to try to change him. Why was it that he tried continually to crowd Christ out of her life?

Robin went downtown that afternoon and made the rounds of the stores applying for work. On the way home she stopped at the supermarket to do her shopping for the rest of the week. She was standing in the center aisle mentally totaling her grocery bill to see if she had money enough for a carton of ice cream when a familiar figure came around the corner. Robin's eyes lit.

"Why Peggy!" she exclaimed. "I didn't expect to see you here."

"Mom sent me down for some milk." She smiled slightly. "How are you these days, Robin?"

"Fine. Both Alex and I have been fine."

"I thought maybe you were away or something," Peggy went on. "I haven't seen you in church for the last month or so."

Hurt flickered in Robin's face. "We went out to the lake a couple of Sundays and–and–." In embarrassment her voice trailed away.

"Dick and I have been wanting to come over and see you kids one of these evenings – if you're going to be at home."

"Dick?" Robin's forehead crinkled. "Who's Dick? Someone new in town?"

Peggy shook her head. "You remember Dick Butler, don't you?"

"Are you going with him?" Robin gasped.

Peggy caught the inflection in her voice and colored slightly. "And just what's wrong with Dick?"

"I–I'm sorry. I didn't mean it the way it must have sounded."

Her friend drew away slightly. "And just how did you mean it?"

"I–I–." She knew that her cheeks were crimson and her thin fingers had begun to tremble.

"It just took me by surprise to hear that you were going with Dick, that's all. I didn't mean to hurt you, Peggy. Please forget that I even said anything about him."

But the other girl's expression did not change. "If you're thinking about the fact that Dick used to drink and smoke, he doesn't do either anymore. He quit them both when I started going with him. Why, he has even gone to church with me a couple of times. And that's something he had never done before."

Robin started to reply, but an elderly woman from the church came up just then.

"Well, well, if it isn't Robin Evans," she said.

The girl managed a weak smile. "Not anymore. My name is Smith now."

Mrs. Gregory's features sharpened. "Your name may be Smith to most people, but you're still Robin Evans to me. Imagine a little thing like you being married when you aren't even old enough to be going with boys. I can't understand what your parents were thinking of that they'd permit it!" She paused significantly. "And that reminds me. I haven't been seeing you in church lately."

Robin squirmed and struggled miserably for words.

"The first time I see that husband of yours I'm going to give him a piece of my mind. These boys always look for a church girl, but they won't go to church themselves after they get married."

For a brief moment her searing gaze bore into Robin's. Then she turned and stomped down the aisle in the direction of the meat cases.

Peggy snickered. "Well, I guess you got told."

But Robin scarcely heard her. "Oh, I hope Mrs. Gregory doesn't say anything to Alex. I've been trying and trying to get him to go to church with me. If she sticks her nose into it, he'll get so mad he'll never go."

"I know just what you mean," Peggy answered. "The last time Dick went to church with me she started in our direction. If I hadn't gotten him out of there quick, she'd have torn into him right there in front of everybody."

The two girls walked toward the check-out stand together. For some reason Mrs. Gregory's outburst had cleared the air between them. "I've been wanting to come over and see you for a long time, Robin. There are so many things I'd like to talk to you about."

The young bride smiled warmly. "Do that, Peggy. I'd love to have you. It would be like old times."

⋆ ⋆ ⋆

Alex found it difficult to get back to studying after being out of school for a number of months, but Robin did everything she could to encourage him. In spite of that, however, there were times when it was all he could do to keep from dropping night school and giving up his plans of preparing himself as a coach.

"I don't know whether I can make it or not," he said on one occasion, discouragement thinly edging his voice.

"Of course you can," Robin told him. "You've been doing fine. Look at your grades."

"But I don't get anything done except work and study. We never have time to go out and have any fun."

She went over and sat on the arm of his chair. "Do you remember what you told me when you said you wanted to get your diploma?" she asked him. "You said that we were going to have to work harder than we've ever worked before. Well, we can't quit before we even get started."

"Four years is such a long time."

She smiled down at him tenderly. "Four years isn't so long when we're working for something as important as your college education."

"Robin," he said, "you're the greatest!"

* * *

Two or three weeks had passed since Robin had seen Peggy Merrill. She had all but forgotten that her friend had said she was going to come over and talk to her, until one December afternoon when there was a knock at the door and she went to answer it. "Why hello, Peggy. Come in.

The other girl stepped inside and closed the door. "I just had to come over and see you," she said.

They sat down across from each other and Robin waited for her friend to speak.

"I suppose it's silly for me to come to you this way," she began, "but I–I've just got to talk to somebody." Her fingers were knotting and untying her head scarf nervously.

"Yes?"

"It's my parents!" Peggy breathed deeply. "They told me I'm not to see Dick anymore."

"Oh."

"I don't know what's the matter with them. I got a low grade in English and they blamed Dick for it and told me that I'm not to date him anymore."

Robin sat there uncomfortably.

"But Dick and I have decided that they can't do that to us! We're going to run away and get married the same as you and Alex did."

Silence hung like a curtain between the two girls. Peggy's face was taut and drawn and her usually mild gray eyes flamed her indignation.

"I–I suppose your parents were thinking of how important it is that you get all your credits so you can graduate with your class," Robin said quietly.

Peggy's temper flared. "Dick and I talked about it

last night." She lowered her voice and leaned forward. "We're going to show them. We're going to get married!"

The color drained from Robin's checks and her lips parted slightly, but she did not speak.

Peggy read the concern in her eyes.

"And what's the matter with you?"

"I was just thinking about what you said."

"But you and Alex are happy – aren't you?"

"Yes, we're happy," Robin said, hesitating slightly. Then, on impulse, she moved her chair closer to that of her friend. "You're the very best girlfriend I've ever had, Peggy," she began. "I'm going to tell you something that I've never told anyone else, if you'll promise not to say anything to anyone about it."

Questions gleamed in her friend's eyes. "I promise."

"Not to Dick, or your parents, or anybody?"

"Not to anybody."

Robin pulled in a deep breath. "I didn't lie to you when I said that Alex and I are happy. And I do love him. But I know that we're not as happy as we could be."

Her young friend frowned seriously. "What do you mean?"

"We don't have any Christian fellowship, for one thing."

"Dick and I have that settled. He's promised to go to church with me every Sunday after we're married. It won't be long until he's a Christian."

Robin smiled knowingly. "That's exactly what I would have said about Alex before we got married.

But Peggy, it hasn't worked out that way. Alex not only won't go to church with me, he won't even let me talk with him about the things of the Lord."

"I'd never thought it was anything like that." Peggy spoke thoughtfully. "I always figured that Dick loves me so much he'd go to church with me and allow me to talk with him about Christ."

"Don't count on his ever becoming a Christian, Peggy," Robin said.

"Don't you think you'll lead Alex to the Lord some day?"

Robin shook her head. "I pray for Alex a dozen times a day," she went on, "but when I stop to think about it, I wonder if God is ever going to answer this particular prayer the way I want Him to. You see, I deliberately turned my back on His will for my life when I gave up His call to full-time Christian service. And I made that decision unchangeable when I married Alex."

Peggy was a long while in answering. "I didn't think I'd hear you say something like this."

Robin laid a hand on her friend's arm. "It hurts me to say this, Peggy, but I can't let you go ahead and get married to someone who isn't a Christian without telling you what it's going to be like. The Bible is certainly true when it says that a believer shouldn't marry an unbeliever. I know. From experience."

"But–." She swallowed hard. "But I *love* Dick."

"I love Alex, too. But I know now that Alex isn't God's first choice for my life." She continued to talk with Peggy. "A person who isn't a Christian has an entirely different set of values. He wants different friends, and he wants to do a lot of things a Christian feels it is better not to do."

As Robin talked Peggy grew even more serious. "You almost make me afraid to get married."

"That's exactly what I'm trying to do," Robin went on. "I'll go even farther than that. I don't think you should even go with Dick anymore."

The other girl straightened slowly. "But I can't do that," she said. "I love him."

Robin nodded. "I'd give a great deal if I had listened when my parents warned me about Alex. I'm sure we'd both be much happier today."

Peggy rose to leave. "You've certainly given me something to think about."

"I'll be praying for you."

Before Peggy could answer there was the sound of footsteps on the stairs and Alex opened the door. "Hi, Peggy."

"Hello, Alex."

He pushed past her to enter the apartment.

"I saw Dick at the station a little while ago. He said he thought you were going to come up to see Robin tonight."

Peggy flushed.

"You wouldn't be thinking about getting married, too, would you?" he asked.

"I–I don't know."

Alex laughed pleasantly. "I told Dick he'd have to bring you over here and have Robin do a selling job on you. She can tell you what it's like being married, can't you, Honey?"

Robin smiled.

* * *

Robin thought often about Peggy and her boyfriend during the next few days. It was not until she met Peggy on the street one afternoon that she learned what had taken place. Although it was cold and there was snow in the air, Peggy stopped her on the sidewalk.

"Oh, Robin, I'm so glad to see you," she said. "I've been wanting to come over to your apartment all week."

"I've been wanting to talk to you, too."

"I'd like to come over now, but I can't. I've got to run." She moved closer and lowered her voice. "But I can tell you that I followed your advice."

Before Robin could reply her friend went on.

"The night after I was at your place, I couldn't sleep at all. I prayed and prayed about Dick and–and–." She swallowed hard. "Finally, I saw that I had to give him up."

Tears welled suddenly in Robin's eyes. "Oh, Peggy!" she exclaimed.

THE DANNY ORLIS SERIES

The Danny Orlis series, by Bernard Palmer, delivers a blend of adventure, mystery, and suspense through various settings—from the Canadian wilderness to Guatemalan jungles. Danny Orlis, an adept outdoorsman, skilled athlete, and committed Christian, employs his quick thinking, calm bravery, and biblical solutions to confront everyday problems and hair-raising dangers. Early stories focus on Danny navigating school life, sports, and outdoor challenges, while in later books, Danny and his wife Kay provide wisdom and guidance to youngsters facing lifelike situations and challenges. Having sold over two million copies, this series has made Palmer a renowned author in Christian youth literature. Palmer is also the author of the Felicia Cartright series and various other series for Christian youth.

AVAILABLE FROM WWW.ANEKOPRESS.COM